The Poppykettle Papers

The Poppykettle Papers

ROBERT INGPEN

—— TEXT BY ——

MICHAEL
LAWRENCE

PAVILION

The vision of El Niño chasing fish in his serpent boat with pelican slaves on
page 2 appears on a 400 year old clay pot made by Inca craftsmen of Peru.
I saw the pot in an archaeological museum in Lima, and copied the picture while
working in Peru in the early 1970s – so began the tale of *The Poppykettle Papers*.

RI

For Abigail Annie Lawrence my beautiful and talented daughter
whose unchosen land awaits.

ML

First published in Great Britain in 1999 by
PAVILION BOOKS LIMITED
London House, Great Eastern Wharf
Parkgate Road, London SW11 4 NQ

Illustrations © Robert Ingpen 1999

Text © Michael Lawrence 1999

Design and layout © Pavilion Books Ltd 1999

The moral right of the author and illustrator has been asserted

Designed by Janet James

A CIP catalogue record for this book is available from the British Library.

ISBN 1 86205 282 4

Set in Bodoni Book

Printed and Bound in Italy by Giunti, Prato.

2 4 6 8 10 9 7 5 3 1

This book can be ordered direct from the publisher. Please contact
the Marketing Department. But try your bookshop first.

CONTENTS

THE FINDING OF THE PAPERS   7

THE FINDING OF THE PAPERS

SOME YEARS AGO, on a sheep farm at Longford in northern Tasmania, two cousins named Rick and Tom were out early on business. It was Easter Sunday and they'd been told that if they were sharp they stood a good chance of finding some chocolate eggs in one of the old barns. The day was as pure as best honey, as golden as a spring dream, quite the opposite of the dank, gloomy interior of the dilapidated old barn, in which a pair of ragged crows sat chattering together in the high rafters. When the boys tumbled in, yelling at the top of their voices, the disgruntled crows flurried off in a huff at the intrusion.

The eggs weren't hard to find, tucked away in the hay, in musty shadows, in twists of rusty old farm machinery. When they reckoned they'd found all there was they made to leave, but then Rick's foot plunged through the floor. His eggs went flying.

'They're yours,' said Tom.

'We said we'd split 'em,' Rick said, extricating his foot.

'Yours already did.'

'Hey, what's that?'

A shaft of brilliant light riddled with dust illuminated the part of the floor he'd gone through. He dropped to his knees; peered into the hole. Tom joined him.

'It's a little box.'

'Brilliant. What's it doing down there?'

'How would I know?'

They clawed at the ground, softened by last night's heavy rain which, like the light, had found a way in through the crumbling roof. They jostled one another, but Tom got to it first, and lifted the box out between finger and thumb. It wasn't just small, it was tiny, and so old that all it took to snap the lock was the jerk of a coin. Inside, they found a few dinky little things and a batch of papers the size of a postage stamp, covered in writing a doll might have made.

They took the box up to the house. Their relatives were intrigued, but even with a magnifying glass they were unable to read the papers. Whatever language they were written in, it wasn't one they knew. They called an archaeologist friend in Launceston, who drove out the following day and was so excited that he personally took the box to the museum at Hobart. The museum people were puzzled by the find and invited a semi-retired specialist in dead languages to examine the papers. The professor returned a few months later with a complete translation, sore eyes and a huge grin. Nothing like this had ever come his way before. He planned to write a book about the papers, but his heart gave out in his sleep six nights later, so instead of making the best-seller lists they were placed within the archive of the Hobart Museum, where they have languished uncelebrated to this day.

The present illustrated volume is the first full translation of the minuscule scraps found by two boys one golden Easter morn when they were looking for other things entirely.

Welcome to The Poppykettle Papers

Aloof's 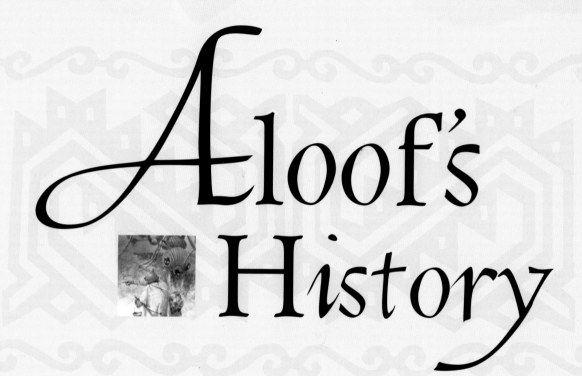 History

A Gift of the Morning Tide

MY PEOPLE ARE DEAD. Murdered. By El Niño. Sixty-eight of us in one night. We five are the last, and I am the youngest. My people live long compared to humans, but when we are gone our kind will have vanished from the face of the earth. I write this so that some day others may know that people of sensible size once lived and breathed upon this shore.

But who were we? *What* were we? It is said that back in the mists of time the Tall Ones (who call this land Peru) fashioned dolls in their own likeness out of driftwood and cloth and human hair. The dolls were intended for sacrifice to El Niño in hope that he would send plenty of fish and spare them the worst of his rages. Well, it seems the dolls amused El Niño, for he breathed life into some of them and called them his little Hairy Peruvians. To each Hairy Peruvian he gave a special Gift, that he or she might have an individual use or purpose. The greatest Gift of all went to one called Adagio, and when the Tall Ones moved away

it fell to him to make new dolls and give them life, and a particular Gift to go with it. He was not a fast worker, that old fellow, and we multiplied slowly over the centuries. There were just seventy-three of us at the end: the night El Niño decided we no longer amused him.

The storm was sudden and terrifying. The stars winked out and the moon fled as the sky became bloated with cloud. Then lightning sprang forth to rile the ocean, and a great wave rose up and rolled against us like a mighty chariot, with the god himself at the helm. He rode us down without mercy or pity, and when his wave-chariot turned about it carried off fifty-nine of us. Of the fourteen that were left, nine were dead, among them Adagio the Maker.

It has been the custom since El Niño's first namings that every Hairy Peruvian name begins with the same letter. This is to show that we are all equal, with no one superior to any other. Only the most ancient is given a title to set him apart, and that title's respect. Our Elder, Don Avante, is one of the survivors. My sister Arnica and I have called Don Avante Grandfather since the day Adagio created her thirty-five years ago and me eight years later. Arnica is the only female left. The other two survivors are also old men. Their names are Astute and Andante. My name is Aloof.

A new day, and an unusual object delivered on the morning tide. I was already up and saw it first: a huge thing with a great round base and an enormous handle and a fat snout. I shouted to the others.

'A human shaving bowl,' Andante said, sitting up with a scowl. 'Thank you,

11

Aloof. I really needed to be woken up to see that.'

'I think it's a poppykettle,' Arnica said, strolling round it.

'A poppykettle?' I regretted it the moment I said it, knowing that a legend was bound to follow. It did. Arnica and her legends.

But it goes like this. Long ago, before the world was flat, the gods fashioned a number of great kettles out of clay and put them in their underground kilns. The kettles were for brewing the poppy tea they were so fond of. But the heat of the kilns was too great and the land cracked and rose up here and there as volcanoes, and the volcanoes erupted and destroyed the world, all except for a single broad shelf surrounded by ocean. Arnica insists that this is one of those kettles.

'I wonder if we could get inside it?' said Astute.

Andante, who is proud to lack Astute's curiosity, stared at him as if he'd mislaid his mind. 'Why would we want to do that?'

'Well, if we could secure the lid and block up the hole in the spout, next time El Niño loses his temper we might live to tell of it.'

'It could serve you better than that,' said another voice.

'Pelé!' Arnica skipped over to the brown pelican, a good friend who often brings us fish when stocks are low. 'Up early aren't you, old fellow?'

'That is no way to address a Venerable Bird.' Yet he allowed her to stroke his beak. Pelé has a soft spot for my sister, don't ask me why.

'What is this other use we could put the kettle to?' Don Avante said.

'Fix a sail to it, fill it with provisions, and it may carry you to a another land
across the ocean – a somewhat safer land.'

Andante snorted. 'Us, sail off in that thing? I don't think so.'

'Why not?' I said.

'Why not? Because, my boy, it would be very dangerous, that's why not.'

'More dangerous than staying here?'

'I should tell you,' said Pelé, 'that I have spoken with El Niño.'

'That's very brave of you,' Arnica said. 'He enslaves pelicans.'

'I am one of the freeborn. He lets all freeborn kinds alone, to wander where they will. He told me that your kind's time in this old land is at an end. A new country awaits you at World's Edge, where the sun goes down.'

'Pity he didn't mention it before wiping most of us out,' I said.

'Aloof!' cautioned Don Avante.

'Did El Niño send the Poppykettle?' Arnica asked Pelé.

'He didn't tell me everything.' But he looked away as he said this, suggesting that he knew more than he was prepared or able to say.

'Well I say we take a chance and go,' I said.

'So do I,' said Arnica.

'I'm embarrassed to admit it,' said Astute, 'but I find myself in agreement with Andante. Adventuring is for the young. Three of us are very old. I'm not sure we could survive a long sea voyage.'

'Yes, let Arnica and Aloof go,' Andante said. 'We'll take our chances here.'

'But you can't!' Arnica cried. 'There are just five of us left, we must stick together, and if El Niño says there's a new country waiting for us out there we must at least try and find it.'

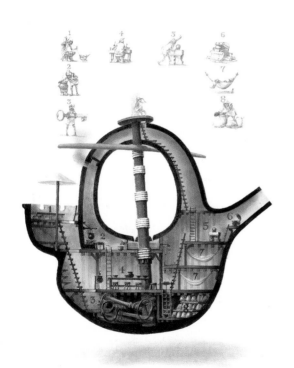

'All very well for you to say,' Andante mumbled. 'You don't have a bad back.'

'Nor do you,' said Astute.

'I'll certainly get one if I go gallivanting across the world.'

'Still, she does have a point. And there's nothing for us here now.'

Astute, Arnica and I turned to Don Avante, who stood gazing thoughtfully out to sea. As Elder, decisions which affect the majority rest with him, but it isn't Don Avante's way to rush such things so we had quite a wait. At last, however:

'If we can make this thing seaworthy,' he said, 'we'll do it. Set sail for World's Edge and see what lies there.'

'But nothing might lie there!' Andante wailed. 'We could simply drop off into... nothingness!'

'We could,' Don Avante replied with a sudden twinkle. 'But what an adventure! When did you last go adventuring, Andante? Can you even remember?'

'I never did,' Andante returned with distaste. 'I like to think I was born with more sense.'

'Well, sensible or not, you're about to change your ways, you old stay-at-home.'

Andante groaned, but it was decided. We are to leave the shore of our creation, our home of untold years, and sail towards World's Edge, where a new land apparently awaits us.

As soon as we've fixed up the Poppykettle.

THE LEAVING

GETTING EVERYTHING READY is proving a much bigger task than we expected, but even Andante sets about it with a will now he's used to the idea, whistling from dawn to darkfall, for our pleasure and his. Andante whistles like no other. That is his Gift. He whistles the moods of the day, the shades of the seasons, the quirks of the elements. When Andante falls silent or sleeps the world seems emptier somehow.

Astute has carved a cork to block up the spout, and we've fixed a sturdy crossbeam to the handle to support a sail. On the sail, Arnica (the artist among us) has painted the image of a great bird to speed us on our way. We've laid a deck area behind the handle, with a hatch and a ladder to sleeping quarters and storage areas below. Don Avante suggests we put sacks of poppyseed in the hold. Not only will their weight keep the kettle from turning over, he says, but we can brew the holy poppy tea in honour of the old gods. 'Perhaps the brewing and sipping will bring us fair weather – and El Niño's blessing. We'll need that.'

16

It came at last, the big day, when we five, feeling rather pleased with ourselves (and rather bold) stood on deck while Pelé towed the Poppykettle out to deeper waters. It was strange to be leaving the shore our people have called home since the dawn of Hairy Peruvian time, but there was too much to look forward to for regret or sorrow.

When we were far enough out to feel the stirring of a good breeze, Pelé wished us fair voyaging. Arnica walked her fingers along his beak. 'Can't you come with us, Pelé? It won't be the same without you.'

'No, no. I'm much too large and heavy for your vessel – and my wings won't carry me as far as you'll be going.'

'Do you think we'll be all right?' she said.

'Why ask me, child? You're the one with the Gift of Prophecy.'

'I know, but...'

My sister is nervous of her Gift and uses it as little as possible for fear of what she might see. But now that it had been thought of, the old men begged her to seek a future for us. 'What better time,' Astute said, 'with the last of our kind about to set forth on such an historic expedition?'

'But what's the *point*?' she protested. 'You know I can never put a date or time on what I see. I might see something really terrible that won't happen for years and years, and we could spend half our lives dreading it happening any minute.'

They didn't like to press her, but they looked so disappointed that she gave in. She seated herself on the deck, closed her eyes and put her fingers to her temples. We leaned over her, eager to hear what future the Ancients would show her.

18

'I see a white pelican,' she said after a while.

I looked at our friend. 'You grown old, Pelé?'

He shook his beak. 'I'm brown today and brown I'll be the day I die. Perhaps the fellow she sees is a relative of different colour.'

'A map now,' Arnica went on. 'A map so big we can walk on it.'

We exchanged glances over her head. A giant map? What could that mean?

'Water,' my sister said.

I was about to say what a wonderful Gift it is that tells seafarers that water lies ahead of them, but Don Avante frowned me into silence.

'A great column of it,' she added. 'Taller than any tree, reaching all the way to the sky, and moving so fast it...'

We waited for more. In vain. She opened her eyes and got to her feet.

'So fast it what?' I said.

'Nothing. That's all there was.'

'You'd better be on your way,' Pelé said, 'or you'll miss the best of the day. Is there anything else I can do for you? No? Farewell then. Remember me.'

We watched him return to the shore on his great slow wings, not without sadness. But then Don Avante was ordering us to let the breeze into our sail and there was no time for sadness, or anything else. We were off!

A QUEST OR TWO

AT FIRST THE KETTLE wobbled badly, but once we'd rearranged the seed sacks in the hold it steadied and proved a worthy craft. Soon we were skimming across the ocean. By nightfall the only land we'd ever known was nothing more than a bumpy line far behind us. Don Avante decreed that someone should always keep watch at night. Arnica volunteered for the first shift and the old men went below. I made my bed on deck, happy to drift off beneath the stars.

It was a very short sleep.

'Aloof! Aloof, wake up!'

I woke. Found Arnica crouching over me.

'Come and look. We seem to have a visitor.'

I struggled out of my blankets and followed her to the side. And stared. 'Is that who I think it is?'

'Who else do you know who travels in a reed boat with a serpent's head at either end?'

20

It was him all right, in physical form, though bearing a brightness unknown to living flesh in the night, coming towards us with his entourage of pelican slaves and flying fish.

'*Small Ones*,' El Niño said almost in a whisper as he drew near, '*I have work for you. Two tasks which serve one purpose.*'

Now it is usual among my people to praise El Niño whatever he does, even when he takes our lives. 'Oh, but he's a god,' we say. 'He must have a *reason*.' Don Avante, Astute and Andante would have fallen to their knees before him. Even Arnica stepped back a pace. But not me. Not now. A rage as hot as flame raced through me.

'You dare give us tasks?' I shouted. 'You, who snatch innocents from their homes and fling them to your salty depths? I defy you, cruel one! Defy you and challenge you! Set aside your godly powers and face me hand to hand. But I warn you, I'll kill you if I can!'

Thunder barked from the cloudless sky, lightning stabbed the water round the Poppykettle, and El Niño... El Niño laughed.

'*Boy, I have only to raise a finger and you are no more.*'

'Then raise it! Do away with me too! It's so easy for you, isn't it? You destroy because you can! How cowardly!'

Arnica dug her fingers in my arm. 'Aloof, what are you trying to *do*?'

I shrugged her off. 'He slaughtered our people! I won't kneel to such a tyrant, even one who calls himself a god!'

As he'd rightly claimed, he could have raised a finger and I'd be gone. I half expected it once his laughter died, but all that happened was that the sky fell quiet and the lightning ceased. When next El Niño spoke he made no reference to my insolence – or my challenge.

'*You are to locate two items. A feather and a dolphin's egg.*'

'What?' I said, too amazed to be grateful that I still had limbs and eyes. 'A feather and an egg? What game is this?'

'*If it is a game, you'll know it by the end.*'

'Why us?' Arnica said, addressing him for the first time. 'Until recently you could have had your pick of Hairy Peruvians to find these things for you.'

'*It may be that you five have the most appropriate Gifts.*'

'Andante's Gift is Whistling,' I snapped. 'What good is that except for lulling and amusing?'

'*We'll see,*' he answered with a smile. '*We'll see.*'

'Why do you hate our people so, El Niño?' Arnica asked him. 'What have we ever done to you?'

'*Hate you?*' He seemed genuinely surprised. '*How can you think that? Who was it gave life to the first of you, and the Gift of Creation to one of your kind?*'

'Yes,' I said bitterly, 'to Adagio, who you recently killed along with all the others.'

He sighed. The waves shifted beneath him.

'*Life. Such a fragile thing. I wouldn't wish it on anyone. But it is the way things are done, and some hold on to it less cleverly than others. I try not to interfere.*'

Then his eyes flashed once more and he looked hard at us.

'*Now listen, and listen well. You will only find peace in the new country I've marked out for you if you claim the feather and the dolphin's egg along the way. The Gift of Prophecy will guide you to the first. The whereabouts of the other is in the knowledge of the lion-face and the dancer.*'

'Who are they?' Arnica said.

El Niño did not answer, or even say goodbye, as he turned his serpent boat about and left us. But his voice returned, fading steadily as he and his courtiers approached the invisible doorway to his world, which stands at the utmost edge of the ocean.

'*Five shall embark and two be lost*
One will race to the Shadows
One will fall to the angry mouth
And three will count the cost.
Three will leap to the meeting ground
Where fear springs at the dark
Where painted past seeks prophecy
And names emerge, undrowned.'

'Now what's that all about?' I said.

Arnica offered no opinion. I looked at her. Her eyes were closed, lips moving silently as she used an old memory-trick of hers, tracing the words into her mind to recall at leisure. When it was done her eyes sprang open with alarm.

'Two will be lost! Aloof! Only three of us will reach the new land!'

'What's all the racket?'

Andante scowled up from the hatch in the deck.

'El Niño was here,' I said.

'What? You've been dreaming, boy!'

'Then I have too,' Arnica said.

Andante clambered up on deck, followed by Don Avante and Astute. They'd heard me shouting – heard me but not El Niño. Gods have ways of making themselves known only to those they choose. Now *there's* a Gift for you!

We told them what had happened and been said and Arnica recited the mysterious verse.

'So we have to find a feather,' Don Avante said, scratching his beard. 'Any particular kind, or...?'

'He said my Gift will guide us to it,' Arnica told him. 'And the dolphin's egg will come to us by way of the lion-face and the dancer – whatever they are.'

'Might be a small problem there,' said Astute. 'I know it's only a detail, but dolphins, you know, don't actually lay eggs.'

We gazed helplessly about us. There were more stars in those fathomless skies than we'd ever seen, and with the ocean as still and clear as a mirror how vast that bright world seemed! Where, in all that, could we hope to find a particular feather and an egg that didn't exist? And why were they so important anyway?

THE SONG THAT KILLS

MY GIFT IS CLEAR SIGHT, which allows me to see further than any other of our kind. I can even see quite well in the dark. Because of this Don Avante has made me chief lookout, and yesterday, after many days on the open sea, I spied an untidy group of small islands. Barely more than rocks they were, not very inviting, but we can't afford to ignore any land, however unpromising, in case the feather or the egg that doesn't exist are there.

We were drawing close to the first of these rocks when a startling thing happened. Part of it rose up, and in rising developed eyes and scales, a great knobbly head, and a crest of spikes that ran the length of its back.

'Dragon!' cried Andante.

'Iguana,' said Astute, who knows everything.

'What shall we do?' Arnica said nervously.

'Jump for it, I say,' Andante replied.

'And meet a nasty end on the rocks?' I said.

'Better than being eaten by that thing.'

He hoiked a leg over the side and would have thrown himself after it if Don Avante hadn't gripped him just above the knee.

'I don't recall giving my permission to abandon kettle.'

Andante withdrew his leg, and bowed. 'Apologies, Don Avante. It was craven fear. I'll be the first to be eaten if you command it.'

'Don't give me ideas,' Don Avante said sourly.

We were now almost within reach of those mighty jaws. The iguana thumped its spiky tail and dipped its bumpy head, all set to dine on Hairy Peruvian. But then the ugly brute breathed a great hot dragon breath that struck our sail and sent the Poppykettle spinning into a lively channel between that island and the next. At first we thought we'd escaped, but then we saw more iguanas on the second island, smaller and brighter in colour than the first; younger and faster. And they'd noticed us. As the Poppykettle bobbed nearer, several of them slipped into the water to investigate.

'*Now* can I jump, Don Avante?' Andante asked politely.

'Right into their slavering jaws? By all means, if that's your wish.'

Andante did not jump. The Poppykettle, tossed this way and that, careered between the islands, watched closely by the young iguanas. Any minute we expected to find ourselves tumbling down one green throat or another. Arnica reached for my hand. I did not refuse it.

29

But they must have been more curious than hungry, for they made no move to snatch us up and swallow us, and the Poppykettle bounced under each scaly nose in turn. And then Andante was whistling his All's-Well Whistle, and the islands of the iguanas were behind us. I shoved Arnica's hand away.

Such a long and tedious time passed then, without the meanest sliver or splinter of land to be seen in any direction, that we lost all track and count of the days. But the sailing was fair and we made good progress — towards what we had no idea, aiming only for World's Edge, which to our surprise always keeps the same distance.

But at last a small pleasant-looking island came into view. I called down to the others. They cheered and rushed to look, and were still cheering when I noticed that almost exactly between us and the island lay a low reef pounded by furious breakers. If we ventured too close to the reef our craft might easily be smashed to pieces, and us with it unless we were lucky enough to drown first. Again I shouted down. Hairy Peruvian cheers turned to Hairy Peruvian groans. Don Avante ordered us to continue on our way rather than attempt to navigate the obstacle, but before we'd gone any distance a wicked wind sprang up and filled the sail, and the Poppykettle reeled helplessly towards the reef.

Then an even more unsettling thing occurred. As it whisked us forward, ever forward, the wind's howl mellowed into a song without words, whose eerie melody writhed like a serpent about my ears, demanding to be heeded. As I listened all fear of reefs and death left me, and a great happiness took its place. I looked

down to see if my joy was shared, and saw the others gazing ahead with eager anticipation. I sought the reef once more, the excellent reef I was to die upon, and noticed that it was surrounded by shifting wreckage. Other happy voyagers must have strayed this way and been lulled to their deaths by the song of the...

No! I punched my way out of my comfortable trance. Unless I acted quickly we would all be killed. I shouted wildly to block out the sound, and slid down the handle. The others, deaf to me, swayed gently to the sly death song. Not daring to let up in my shouting for an instant, I freed a rope at a sail corner and tugged, hoping to change our course. The wind, angered, slapped the sail, causing the rope to jerk me into the air, crack like a whip, fling me away. I hit the waves, went under, turning slowly over and over, going down, down, down...

But then: something broad and firm beneath me, bearing me up again, and suddenly the ocean burst like a great bubble and I sat gasping in the palm of a colossal hand, while a pair of huge eyes examined me. I think I fainted.

THE AP

I LAY ON A BEACH of warm white sand beside a sparkling lagoon. The sun beat down, but a fine breeze teased the leaves of leaning palms. I lifted my head. The Poppykettle had been hauled onto the beach and the others stood with the human female who had lifted me from the water. Around her neck she wore a necklace of barnacles, and beside her lay a net crammed with fish so enormous that I counted myself lucky not to be waking in one of their bellies.

'Well!' Arnica said. 'Aloof, back in the land of the living! Trust you to sleep through everything. You might like to know that if not for this Tall One we'd be part of the reef by now.'

'And I'll have *you* know,' I said, sitting up, 'that I was the only one to keep his wits out there while you...'

She wasn't listening. Wouldn't have believed me anyway. The human female glanced at me but did not smile. Her face was so lined it would probably have cracked if she had. I got up and approached, taking care to keep well out of her reach.

'Are you sure she can be trusted?'

'Saved our lives,' Andante said. 'Needn't have bothered.'

'What have you learned about her?'

'Enough to know that she wishes us no harm,' Astute said.

I should mention that Astute's Gift is Wisdom, which besides great knowledge includes the ability to make sense of the words and calls and cries of almost every creature that has a voice, the great and the small, the fleet and the slow, the winged and the finned. The only creatures the rest of us can understand are pelicans, because those noble birds have been our friends and providers through all our existence. We would have been dull indeed not to have learned their speech, as they learned ours.

'She tells me,' Astute went on, 'that she lives here with a few others of her race, that she was swimming underwater looking for fish when she saw the Poppykettle in trouble, and...'

He stopped because the woman had risen without a word and walked away.

'Her manners leave something to be desired,' Don Avante said gruffly as she entered a cave at the back of the beach.

I looked about me. It was a very pleasant spot. 'Manners or not,' I said, 'if all the natives are as friendly as her we could do worse than make our home here.'

'Hardly,' Arnica said. 'There are things we must find before we settle anywhere.'

'A feather and an egg?' I flung my hands at the sky. 'Look: birds! Birds have feathers! Birds lay eggs!'

'They don't lay dolphins' eggs,' she said scornfully.

'Nor do dolphins,' I reminded her.

'And it can't be just any feather. El Niño said my Gift would lead us to the feather. I've looked into my mind. There's nothing there.'

'I could have told you that without any Gift,' I said, and ducked a sisterly swipe.

'We couldn't stay here anyway,' Don Avante said. 'Look what she doodled in the sand while she was talking.'

The casual drawing showed several large stick figures chasing a handful of much smaller ones and roasting them over an open fire.

'How do we know *she* doesn't plan to do that?' I said. 'Maybe she's gone to stoke up the fire to cook us over with the fish.'

Andante glanced uneasily towards the cave at the very instant the woman emerged. He paled. 'She's coming back! And she has a weapon! Aloof's right, she's going to kill us!'

It wasn't a weapon. Reaching us she unfurled it on the sand; an odd thing, made up of sticks tied together with vines, dotted with cowrie shells. There was no pattern to it. She pointed at a shell near the middle and spoke in her strange tongue. Astute translated.

'She says it's a map of the region. The shell at the centre is this island, the others are neighbouring islands.'

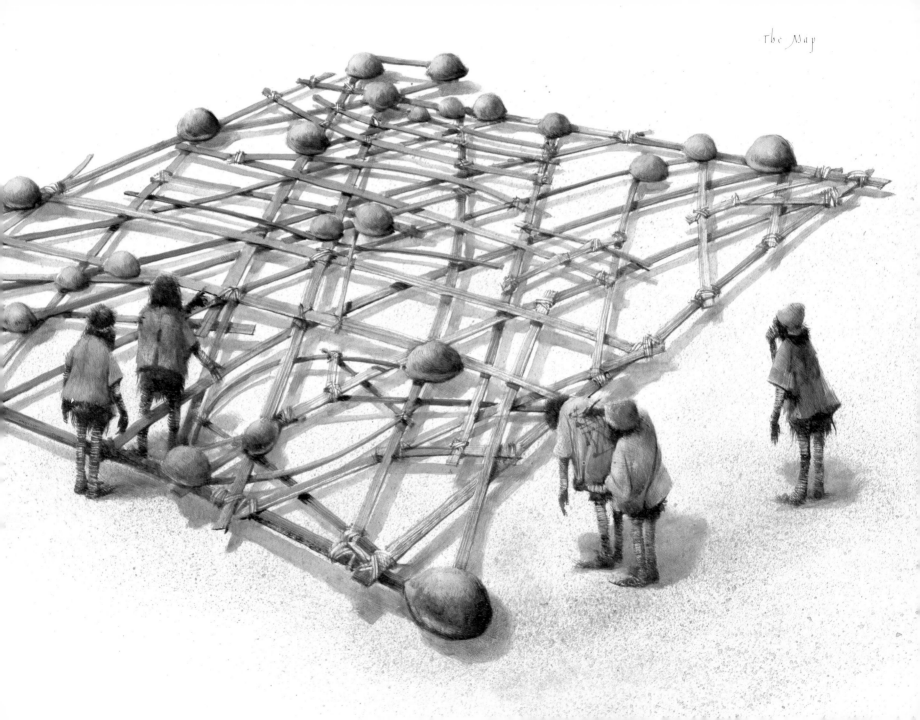

Don Avante leant over the map with interest. 'Look at the way the sticks bend and cross. I do believe they're placed in such a way as to show the currents and wind directions hereabouts. I'm impressed.'

Now the Tall One trailed a slow finger around and between the islands, ending up at the edge of the peculiar map.

'She's showing us which way to go,' Astute said. 'The course to set if we're to avoid the worst hazards.'

'Might still be a trick,' Andante said from behind Arnica. 'Watch out she doesn't throw the map over us, bundle us up and cart us off to the cooking pot.'

The old woman lit a fire all right, but not to cook us over. She baked some of the fish she'd caught and shared one with us. One was enough. When we'd eaten, Arnica copied the map onto the back of Andante's shirt. He protested, mainly because he was still wearing it, but Don Avante told him to be quiet. We then climbed onto the Poppykettle and the woman carried us across the lagoon and the reef (where the wind no longer sang) and set us on our way with a puff or two of very fishy breath.

Volcano!

IN ALL PROBABILITY Don Avante, whose Gift is Navigation, would have been able to steer us away from there without the map; but it gave him pleasure to jab at Andante's back with a sharp finger end while tracing a course on his shirt. One of the hazards we most wanted to avoid was the Island of the Volcano, which the old woman had taken pains to warn us about. We sighted it one afternoon a day or two after leaving her lagoon. Smoke and flames leapt from the volcano's mouth and lava rolled down the near side in thick waves, covering the scattered dwellings on the slope and all else that lay in its path. Don Avante's course put us on a brisk current that would carry us clear of the island. We were proceeding well when we spied a broad sail beyond the rising breakers to our left, then a number of Tall Ones paddling furiously.

'Some of the islanders off to look for a safer home?' I said.

'Like us,' said Arnica.

'Like us?' Andante repeated, feigning astonishment. 'Do they seem of sensible size to you, Arnica? Amazing. To me they seem of very *unsensible* size. Very *unsafe* size. Any one of their kind, as they seem to *me*, could squash us with a thumb or drown us with a single tear. But perhaps I've misunderstood them all these years. Perhaps I -'

He might have gone on in this vein for some time if a sudden dip in the waves had not revealed more of the vessel and its occupants. It was an odd craft, with two carved hulls bridged by a wooden platform crowded with humans casting frightened glances back at the island. It seemed likely that they would be far too intent on their escape to take notice of a floating kettle, but then one of them saw us, gave a shout, and every eye turned our way. Then the craft itself changed direction.

'Get below!' Don Avante hissed.

Andante didn't need telling twice, or even once, for he was already slithering head-first into the hatch, and in his haste passed down the ladder without pausing to set foot on it. Astute wasn't much more cautious, or Don Avante either when Arnica waved him on. At any other time I might have howled myself senseless at the sight of three old men in a tangled heap at the foot of a ladder.

'What are you waiting for?'

Arnica wore that smug Big Sister look of hers which annoys me so much. 'You,' I said. 'I'll see to the hatch.'

She smirked but climbed down, then I too descended, securing the hatch just in time, for almost at once the kettle was seized and turned on its side and I was flung from the ladder while tools and provisions and Hairy Peruvians tumbled in all directions at once.

We cowered where we landed while curious Tall Ones examined our vessel and one of them began stabbing at the hatch with a gigantic finger. We pressed back in terror. If that finger broke through and poked about down here we'd be done for.

'Oh, this cannot go *on*!'

Don Avante leapt from his place of concealment and stalked as purposefully as he could across the skewed floor.

'Where are you going?' Astute said.

'I'm going up to talk to them.'

'Talk to them? How, with sign-language?'

'With anger! I've lived too long at the brunt of El Niño's temper to fall quietly to a bunch of overgrown louts. We are the last of our kind, Astute. Would you have us crushed so easily?'

'Well if you put it like that...'

Astute joined Don Avante at the ladder. I caught Arnica's eye. We both stepped forward. Andante, clutching a sack of poppyseed, made no move to follow our example.

Don Avante was about to step onto the first rung when I saw what I must do. I reached past him, jumped onto the ladder. 'I'll see them off!'

'Don't be ridiculous!' Don Avante snapped. 'Slip of a boy like you, mere twenty seven years of age, they'll laugh at you. No, a person of maturity and authority is needed here.'

'Yes, but not you,' Astute said. 'I'm the only one who stands the remotest chance of -'

'Wait!' Arnica said. 'They've stopped trying to break in. And we're not being tipped up any more.'

I shinned up the ladder, peered through a crack in the hatch. 'Can't see them. Can't see anything, just sky.'

'Surely they can't have gone so quickly,' Don Avante said.

I threw the hatch back, stuck my head up, and immediately wished I'd been more cautious. The Tall Ones, having more pressing business, had set the kettle down, but they hadn't yet gone – and they saw me. I climbed up on deck. Don Avante was next up, then Arnica and Astute. The islanders, who had been staring at us open mouthed, now began to murmur among themselves. Some, I noticed, were trembling badly.

'Can you make out what they're saying?' Don Avante asked Astute.

'Some. They seem to think we're... demons of some sort.'

As if to prove it one of the men reached out, grabbed the Poppykettle, raised it above his head, and with a mighty bellow hurled it from him. Too shocked for words, or even sounds, we clung to one another as we flew far from our safe current, to fall eventually upon a far less friendly tide which conveyed us promptly to the very place we'd set out to avoid. Then the Poppykettle was tossing and spinning on sizzling water, boiled at a touch by lava pouring into it from the shore. The heat here was intense, the fumes overpowering, but luck – if luck it

was – hadn't quite deserted us, and a wave whipped up by the molten stream bore our craft along the lip of the land to gentler, cooler shallows, where it lodged as if unwilling to go further.

I climbed down the bowl of the kettle and waded up to a beach of coarse black sand. A broad band of jungle at the back of the beach was all that stood between us and the volcano, but we seemed safe enough here. It was that other shore, the one we'd left without any wit or skill of our own, to which the lava ran.

The others joined me – even Andante once he'd summoned the courage to quit his hiding place. 'Arnica,' Don Avante said. 'I think you must try and see what lies before us. Whatever it is, even if it's not good, it might help if we have some foreknowledge here.'

For once making no protest, Arnica seated herself and closed her eyes to seek contact with the Ancients who give her glimpses of the way ahead. Moments later all colour drained from her face.

'Talons,' she said.

'What?' said I.

'Talons, scales, eyes like pools of blood. Evil.'

Andante cleared his throat. 'E... evil?'

'It is the one. It has the feather. It's here.'

She shivered violently, tearing herself away from her vision.

'Your prophecies get shorter and shorter.' She looked at me with the eyes of one who has seen terrible things. 'Anyway,' I said, 'what makes you so sure the feather's here? You don't usually have the faintest idea if

you've seen a near future or a far.'

'This time I know,' she answered bleakly. 'We must climb the volcano and take a feather from the creature that lives inside it.'

There was a muffled groan from Andante, who stepped back a pace.

'But what is it, Arnica?' Astute asked. 'A bird of some kind, I imagine, as it has feathers.'

'Of some kind.' She compressed her lips, refused to say more.

'Whatever it is,' said Don Avante, 'bird or rodent or monster from hell, if it has the feather we have to go after it.'

'I'll stay here and mind the Poppykettle,' Andante said. 'I know it's risky, but someone ought to.'

Don Avante scowled at him. 'We've been charged to fetch this damned feather and fetch it we will. All of us, together. I daresay the kettle will still be here when we get back.'

'We may not get back,' Andante pointed out.

'Then we won't need it, will we. Come on, jump to it!'

Andante muttered into his beard but fell in with the rest of us as we headed for the jungle – and the volcano home of the creature we must steal a feather from. A creature which scared my sister to bits.

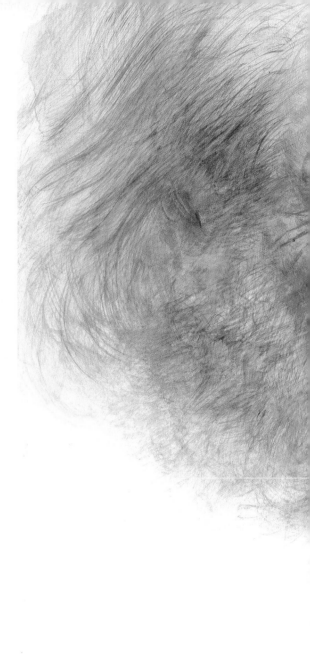

Warnings

THE JUNGLE WAS QUIET enough as we approached it, but once inside we found the silence absolute, as if an order had gone out that no sound be made on pain of death. Yet there was life there, a great deal of it. Picking our way through the towering overgrowth we felt a myriad invisible eyes watching us from root and burrow and branch. As most land creatures are bigger than us and likely to snatch anything that happens innocently by, it was a nerve-racking trek. But no predator pounced, and eventually we were through to the other side and gazing up the slope of the volcano we had no choice but to climb.

After a short rest and some refreshment we began our ascent. We had not gone far when we came upon a red ant gathering food among the rocks. It made a series of sharp angry-sounding noises which were meaningless to all ears but Astute's, who told us that the ant did not seem pleased to see us.

'Probably because we're not ants,' said Andante.

'Astute,' Don Avante said, 'ask it if it's seen our bird-creature.'

'How do I describe it?'

'As terrifying,' said Arnica with a shudder.

Astute began a series of clicks that obviously meant more to the ant than to us, because before he'd finished it reared up, jaws clacking wildly, and loped rapidly away.

'He told us to go no further if we value our lives,' Astute said.

'Interesting,' said Don Avante.

Being the youngest and most agile, Arnica and I took the lead most of the way, hauling the old ones up after us. It was a slow and difficult hike, mostly through rocks and coarse scrub. At one point we came across something odd lying on the ground by some bushes. Long and thick and grey it was, like an eyeless, mouthless snake. Don Avante nudged it with his toe, and it shivered as though woken suddenly and withdrew into the bushes. Then the leaves shook as something bulky turned round within, and a pair of nervous eyes stared out at us.

'Oh, it's only a mouse,' Arnica said.

'A very large mouse,' Andante said, keeping his distance.

Arnica offered a hand to the mouse to show we meant no harm. It cringed, but then, perhaps noticing that it had more bulk than us, came out a bit further. Arnica stroked it, made soothing noises.

Don Avante told Astute to ask the mouse about the feathered one we sought. 'But choose your words with care. Remember the ant. I suggest you praise it first to get it on our side. Tell it it's the most beautiful mouse we've seen today. It's no lie. Say that it has the bright eyes of the knowing and ask if it would be so very kind as to advise us.'

Astute made these overtures to the mouse, which fluttered its eyes coyly in return. But when he asked after the creature we were looking for, it twitched, and such a confused chattering came from it that even he had trouble making something of it.

'I *think* it said that the island is in the creature's thrall, and that even if the volcano were not exploding fear would rule here.'

'Calm it down, get as much as you can out of it,' Don Avante said.

Astute calmed the mouse and questioned it further. The mouse whispered a fearful reply with many an upward glance towards the mountain's flaring summit, as if afraid of being overheard.

'The way he describes it,' Astute said, 'our creature seems to be some sort of cross between an owl and an eagle, with some reptilian features, talons that love tearing flesh, few feathers (purple, by the way) and huge leathery wings.'

An agitated clattering noise came from behind us: Andante's teeth.

'Does it have a name, this beast?' Don Avante asked.

Again Astute consulted the mouse, again the mouse replied.

'He calls it the Cunmerrie,' Astute informed us. 'According to him the Cunmerrie is a creature born of flame whose eyrie is tucked inside the very mouth of the volcano.'

'El Niño's verse!' Arnica said suddenly.

'What about it?' I said.

'*Five shall embark and two be lost*

One will race to the Shadows

One will fall to the angry mouth

And three will count the cost.'

'It might not mean a volcano's mouth,' Astute said.

'And it might,' Andante murmured, and began whistling one of his Comfort Whistles.

'Whether it does or not,' said Don Avante, 'we must press on. Without that feather we'll never find the new land.'

'El Niño didn't say we need the feather to *find* the new land,' Arnica said. 'Only that we'll never know peace there unless we claim it along the way.'

'And the egg,' Astute said with a thin smile. 'Don't forget the non-existent egg.'

We turned to the mouse to thank it, but it had already tucked itself back in the bushes – all except for its tail.

THE TERRIBLE CUNMERRIE

WE CLIMBED ON, higher and higher. As the light began to fade Don Avante ordered us to make camp for the night. We lit a small fire within a circle of stones and prepared a meal from the poppyseeds we'd brought with us, and some fruit and vegetables gathered along the way. We'd hardly finished eating when the old men's eyes began to droop. 'We must keep watch through the night,' Don Avante said wearily. 'We'll take it in turns, five short watches before dawn so that we may all get a decent rest. I'll take first watch.'

'No you won't,' Arnica said. 'You need to build your strength for tomorrow, Grandfather. So do Astute and Andante. I'll take the first half of the night, Aloof can do the rest.'

'Oh thanks,' I said.

While the rest of us settled down by the fire, Arnica clambered up onto a large boulder above us, from where she said she could see all there was to see. Night

came quickly then, and soon I was the only one awake by the fire, trying to decide which was worse, the endless noise of the volcano or the fitful snores of old men. But even I must have fallen asleep eventually because it seemed hardly any time at all before Arnica was shaking me and telling me to be quiet and not wake the others. She took my place by the last of the fire while I climbed wretchedly up to the boulder. The stars were still bright, but there were fewer of them now and the sky was lightening low in the east, which meant that Arnica had either kept watch for longer than she needed to or had dozed off at her post. I wasn't yet fully awake myself, and as there was nothing to do or look at, drowsiness again overtook me.

I was woken by the worst sound I've ever heard, a nightmarish shriek that ripped the silence to shreds and scattered it upon the wind. I stumbled to my feet in alarm as a pair of vast black wings blocked out the last stars and the volcano's fiery glow. I would have jumped down to join the others but the creature was too quick, and suddenly I stood between its dreadful talons staring up into the twin pools of blood that were its eyes. Still it screeched, so piercingly, so horribly, that I could do nothing but shriek back as the cruel beak reared open to take me.

But then something unexpected happened. Perhaps my own racket startled it, for the brute paused before striking and in that pause an unexpected movement caught its murderous eye. Distracted, the Cunmerrie blinked, then snatched up a green lizard scurrying just a little too slowly into a crevice near my feet. If I hadn't left my wits down by the fire I would have seized that moment to roll off the boulder and tuck myself out of sight; but as the Cunmerrie propelled itself from the rock I jumped after it without thought, decision or ambition, and clung

to it. My feet left the ground and the monster gave a squawk of pain as the part I gripped came away in my hands. It might have turned on me, but it did not. It had what it had come for, its terrified, squirming breakfast, and off it flew with it towards its home inside the volcano. As I fell back onto the rock, scales from the beast's reptilian skin rained down on me.

'Aloof?' A voice from below. 'You all right?'

'I... yes. I think so.'

'What's that you've got there?'

Only now realizing what I'd torn from the Cunmerrie I laughed, and bounded down with my prize. Praise came thick and fast from all but Arnica who, examining the great feather in the growing light, wondered how a thing of such beauty and softness could come from such a devilish being. Don Avante, Astute, Andante and I had other things on our minds. The first part of El Niño's task was accomplished! We had the feather! *We had the feather!*

'But what do we do with it?' Andante said as we calmed down.

'I think,' said Don Avante, 'that the best thing we can do is get it back to the Poppykettle and wonder about that later.'

There were no arguments. We gathered ourselves together and started down – with some haste.

DEATH OF AN ISLAND

IT WOULD HAVE TAKEN us almost as long to get back to the beach by way of the treacherous downward slope as it had to climb it if not for a chance meeting along the way. He was a goanna, Astute told us after an exchange of noises, a relative of the lizard the Cunmerrie had carried off to its lair, and pleased to assist any who wished to escape the 'devil bird' as he called it. Climbing on the goanna's back with the feather we continued down at a much happier rate.

We were travelling along the edge of a sheer precipice, rejoicing in our first sight of the black beach far below, and the Poppykettle nestling in the shallows, when a deafening roar made us jump almost out of our skins. Looking back we saw flames leaping from the volcano's mouth and fiery billows of lava rolling after us like an angry pursuer determined to overtake us.

'Go, goanna, go, go, faster, faster!'

This from Andante, an urging echoed by me. The goanna got a move on, but he began to shake so hard that we had to dig our heels in to keep from falling off. He knew as well as we did that he would never outdistance the lava with us on his back. My soft-hearted sister told him to forget about us and make his escape. The goanna seemed to like her suggestion, for he leaned sharply to one side – the side that contained land fortunately – and we tumbled off. With a garbled apology, which received a garbled translation from Astute, he darted into a nook that seemed far too narrow for his broad body.

'Perhaps we should follow him,' I said.

'No,' Astute said. 'That is a lizard's path. Lizards can slither and contract, Hairy Peruvians can't. We'd soon be trapped or cut off or crushed by falling rock.'

The lava, rolling after us in great gallumphing waves, was already so close that we could feel its heat. Our precipitous path rose to a small plateau before falling steeply again, and we hurried to it hoping the lava stream would go round it. It did, at first. We huddled together on the little island in a lake of swirling amber, choking on fumes, blistered by heat, but safe for that minute or two before the lava began to rise. Then Arnica had the bright idea that helped me forgive her for inviting the goanna to abandon us.

'The feather!' She dragged the Cunmerrie's feather to the edge of the rock, below which there was nothing, nothing at all, for a very long way. 'Quick, climb on!'

'How can sitting on a feather preserve us from these fires of hell?' Andante wailed.

'Even a feather this size must be lighter than air,' Arnica replied. 'Unless our weight is too much, it may carry us to safety.'

'And we may drop like five stones.'

'Aloof, get on, at the front!'

She was doing it again, bossing me around, but this was not the moment to put her in her place. I planted myself astride the feather and Don Avante seated himself behind me, followed by Astute, then a very twitchy Andante. Glancing back I saw Arnica grip the shaft. She was about to give it a shove when a tongue of lava slurped over the rock and licked her heel. She yelped, kicked out, her sandal shot into the air in flames, and the feather slipped sharply forward, dipping so steeply that I would have fallen off if Don Avante hadn't grabbed me by the collar and almost strangled me as he hauled me back.

'Get *on*, Arnica!' Astute shouted. 'We need your weight at the back – *now!*'

She jumped on. The front of the feather lifted and Don Avante let go of my collar. Arnica jabbed at the rock with her feet. The feather jerked forward. I grabbed the shaft within the purple fronds. She kicked the rock once more. The feather sailed out into empty space – with a cargo of screaming Hairy Peruvians.

Well we survived, of course we did, or I wouldn't be writing this. Perhaps El Niño was watching over us because he wanted the feather, for a wind-ladder was flung our way to carry us down rung by rung to the very place we wished to be. It was no soft landing – the sand was very coarse – but this was a small price to pay. The lava was gurgling down the slope at an alarming rate now.

'The Poppykettle!' Don Avante bawled, and set off at such a pace that I

wondered what those old legs of his were made of.

Arnica, dragging the Cunmerrie feather, followed at a fast hobble in her one sandal. Astute passed her, splashing into the shallows after Don Avante. Then these two, the oldest of us, scrambled up the side of the kettle with the speed of young children. Once they were on deck Arnica passed the feather to them before also climbing up. In the water, I stood aside to allow Andante to precede me. He started up – but then stopped as though struck by an arrow from behind.

'Someone's got to push us off. Like Arnica did with the feather.'

'All right. Up you go then, but hurry.'

'No,' he said. 'I'll do it.'

'*You?*'

'Yes, me, what's wrong with that?'

'Well, it's just that you usually...'

'Mm. Well we can't all be brave.'

He stepped down and I climbed up, amazed. Andante the hero? Whatever next? He put his back to the kettle and pushed, grunting hoarsely to our shouts of encouragement. It didn't budge. Arnica jumped down to help him, which of course meant that I had to do likewise, but even with our combined strength we might not have managed to push the kettle out of the shallows if the tide hadn't been on the turn. The waves flipped over, rolled back, and soon we were waist-deep in the water with the Poppykettle leaning before us, eager to be gone. We climbed up. Don Avante and Astute had fixed the sail, and we'd barely gained the deck before our craft hurtled away. We gave a ragged cheer and looked back at the island that had almost claimed us.

The lava, now covering the entire slope we'd camped upon, must have reached the edge of the jungle on the far side, for birds that had been silent since our arrival leapt up like spears, silent no longer, while wingless creatures began to emerge from lower cover. As the lava ploughed through the jungle, all the luscious greenery within exploded into flame and the land-based creatures whose home it had been scampered or waddled or slithered into the water, the only place left to them. Most were not swimmers and drowned quickly. The birds that had leapt so frantically from their nests and branches were joined by others, so many others that soon they filled the sky like locusts, tumbling and shrieking and crashing dizzily into one another in their panic.

We were some way out when there came such an almighty crash that we thought the end of the world must be upon us. It was the volcano, riven by its own impossible heat, cracking apart like a clay pot – like a poppykettle.

And the island began to sink.

It wasn't till the upper portion of the volcano was all that stood above the water that the Cunmerrie appeared. It must have been slumbering peacefully inside that molten mouth after its lizard snack, disturbed only when it felt its home subsiding. But it was up now and standing on the rim, shocked by the sight that met its blood-red eyes. Suddenly it gave a shriek so dreadful, so piercing in its misery and rage, that the thousands of ordinary birds that had taken to the skies put their wings to work without delay and took off for North, for South, for East and West, never to stray this way again.

Then there was nothing but bubbling water for the Cunmerrie to stand upon. In spite of its mighty wingspan it can't have been much of a flyer, for it made no attempt to leave and seek haven elsewhere. A creature of the volcano, it could live nowhere else, and when the sea poured into the volcanic mouth a cascade of steam hissed about it, scales flew from it like burning coals, and the terrible Cunmerrie spread its leathery wings like a vast black cloak, threw back its head in a final mournful screech, and disappeared beneath the waves.

Arnica's History

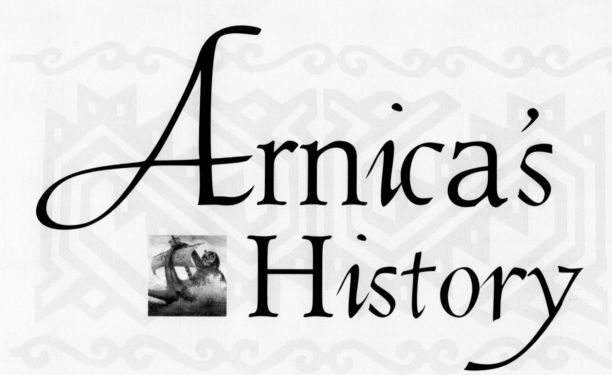

THE FIRST LOSS

ALOOF IS DEAD. There, I've said it. It's written. My brother, my angry difficult little brother, is gone. Forever. I accept it because I must, and move forward. That is my people's way. We don't dwell on the past, merely take from it that which might be of some future use. The present may be recorded, however, so I take up my pen where Aloof left off. This is what happened.

After leaving the Island of the Volcano we fixed the Cunmerrie feather to the highest point of the handle, near Aloof's lookout place. He was up there bringing his record of events up to date when he saw something and shouted down to us.

'Storm coming!'

It wasn't a full-blown storm, no more than a concentrated squall really, a large low cloud gliding towards us with lightning darting from it, making the water jump where it struck.

'It's him!' Aloof cried then. 'El Niño, come for his feather!'

'Can you see him?' I yelled.

'No, but he's in there, I know he's in there!'

'Better get down, Aloof!' Don Avante shouted.

'No! I'm handing it to him personally! I want to look him in the eye and see gratitude there!'

He set about unfastening the knots that tied the feather. By the time he'd got it free, the squall was almost upon us.

'Arnica, hang on to this for me!'

He threw down his papers, held together by a wooden clamp of his own devising. They landed at my feet. I stooped for them, and when I looked up again Aloof was standing on the handle holding the feather over his head with both hands. Just then a skewer of lightning shot from the cloud, missing his ear by a whisker and throwing him off-balance. Aloof swayed, toppled sideways still holding the feather, and then it was carrying him, dangling below it, towards the storm-cloud.

'Let go!' I screamed.

He didn't let go. Of course he didn't, he was Aloof the Bold, Aloof the Reckless, Aloof the Unbelievably Stupid. He just laughed and kicked his legs as if he was off on some delicious new adventure. Still gripping the feather he plunged into the cloud, which enveloped him eagerly and at once swept away, leaving nothing behind, nothing at all but the Poppykettle and four horrified Hairy Peruvians.

Andante was the first to find voice. 'So. He has his feather. El Niño has his feather.'

'He also has Aloof,' Don Avante said sorrowfully, and covered his face. 'Oh my boy, my dear boy. Gone to the shadows.'

'Five shall embark and two be lost,' I said, dashing at my eyes.

'And there's to be another of us before this is done,' said Astute. 'Well then.' He raised his arms to the sky as if to pull it down upon him, and, with great passion, cried: 'El Niño! Take me: Astute! Gather your second victim now and spare these others! If you have a shred of pity get this over with!'

But the wind stayed calm, the waters did not churn, and El Niño did not take Astute. Nor did he return Aloof to us.

A Dancer In Cloud

DAYS PASSED, long lonely wretched days in which I kept much to myself. Understanding my need the others left me to it, and a heavy silence lay upon the Poppykettle as we continued our journey. Andante even ceased to whistle, though he was undoubtedly relieved that we had left behind the last of the islands on the map, for it meant that his back was no longer prodded at every turn. Lacking any knowledge of the way ahead, Don Avante aimed the spout of the kettle at the precise point of World's Edge where the sun sets. Sea birds are the best indication of land, keeping always within reach of it so they can nest or rest their wings from time to time. No birds means no landing place and we saw none for so long that we began to think we'd walked our last firm ground. It occurred to me that the map might have ended where it did because there is nothing more in all this great ocean, but I dismissed this. El Niño had as good as promised us another country. Cruel he sometimes is, but he has nothing to gain by lying to us.

On a certain day, while my companions whittled pieces of wood or trimmed their beards or otherwise occupied themselves, I stood gazing up at a solitary cloud passing overhead. My eyes absently traced the band of fleecy white, seeing nothing in it for a long time, until a shape that had begun to form on one side sharpened my gaze.

'A dancer!'

Everyone jumped. 'Dancer?' Don Avante said. 'What do you mean, Arnica?'

'The cloud, look, where it's breaking up. Legs... feet... *dancing*!'

'What of it?'

'Have you forgotten the dancer that's to lead us to the dolphin's egg?' I cried. 'The dancer and the lion-face. Well why shouldn't they come in a cloud? Oh, and look now, just there! A lion. It must be!'

'Looks like a hat to me,' said Astute.

'I don't even know what a lion is,' said Andante.

'Nor do I,' said I, 'but that doesn't mean it *isn't* one.'

We stood watching and watching until the shapes in the cloud lost all resemblance to a dancer, or a possible lion, or anything else, becoming a featureless filmy strand once more.

There were no recriminations for raising their hopes. They simply returned to their various occupations, quietly. No one said as much, but it was plain to all (including me) that I'd been looking for signs that did not exist; not here, not today, and certainly not in the sky.

THE HAUNTED ISLAND

SURPRISINGLY, the spout of the Poppykettle has proved one of its most useful features. On especially warm days and nights we remove the cork so that a breeze flows into the bowl and cools the air below decks. The neck of the spout has become my favourite place not only to keep lookout but to write and think and be alone. In all my thinking I try not to dwell on Aloof, who I miss more than I (or he) would ever have dreamed pos-

Translator's note

We may never know what The Haunted Island was, or what befell our voyagers there, because from this point a large part of the original document has been virtually destroyed by damp and time, the writing rendered illegible. All we can know with certainty of this period is that the Poppykettle sailed some considerable distance, so that we catch up with it some weeks later when Arnica, the current writer of the History, is once again plunged into despair over the loss of a companion or loved one – a loss that has yet to happen...

THE WATER DEVIL

IT IS EVENING. The sun has slipped over World's Edge and the sky is ablaze with crimson and spun gold. A glorious sight, but I am too filled with misery to enjoy it, for I have seen something I would give all my senses to forget. I have seen which of us is to be the second to die.

I had been settled on deck making some drawings of the others, something I often do when at a loose end, and had just finished a portrait of Astute when he prevailed upon me to seek a future for us. I was in a good mood, the picture was very pleasing, so I sat down, closed my eyes, and called upon the Ancients to guide me to a future of their choosing.

When I felt their presence I groped my way through the darkness. It is sometimes a minute or two before I see anything in my trance state, but this time the interior world was quickly illuminated and a small segment of the future began to play itself out for me. I heard the others questioning me in the distance,

69

but I was too puzzled by what I saw to answer. When the terrible thing happened I must have cried out, for suddenly there were arms about me and soothing words in my ear and when I opened my eyes Don Avante was cradling me and trying to calm me. I took his hand and kissed it repeatedly while my tears fell upon it.

'What is it, Arnica? What did you see?'

I couldn't tell him. Tell anyone. I kept it to myself, locked away inside, where I weep in private.

We heard it before we saw it, a dreadful roaring, whooshing, hissing sound, and then water was pattering down on us like sudden rain.

'What the devil is it?' Andante said.

'A devil indeed,' Astute replied. 'A water devil unless I'm much mistaken. Nothing in their path escapes, and this one... this one seems to be heading our way.'

'Arnica,' Don Avante said, 'just before we left the old shore, didn't you foresee something of this description?'

'Yes,' I said.

'Did it harm us in any way?'

'I don't know. I saw it only as we see it now, then the Ancients showed me something else.'

The column of white water rose from the sea, all the way to the high heavens, where it widened into a broad funnel shape. Moving at an alarming rate, and spinning constantly, it seemed to suck up the water all round it, and all that it

contained. It was still some way off when it began to drag the Poppykettle towards it.

'Excuse me!'

Andante shot down the ladder to the relative safety of the hold. I glanced at the others to see if they were tempted to follow. Not Astute. Astute will risk almost any danger if he thinks there's some knowledge to be gained at the end of it. Don Avante appeared equally fascinated by the whirling pillar, transfixed by it as it hauled us towards it. Spray drenched us as it caught the kettle, and then we were travelling upward in the company of thousands of startled fish, upward and inward through the spinning wall of water.

Now we were through and climbing the inner wall. The thing was hollow. The sound was different inside. A deafening high-pitched scream like a hundred Cunmerries all shrieking at once. It was stifling too, and smelled of rotting seaweed. I saw below an immense circle of churning ocean, while high above, where the column fanned out, a filigree of lightning bolts formed a shimmering canopy over all. There was no way of telling how long or far the water devil had travelled, but it had picked up many other things before reaching us, and carried them still. Apart from all the fish, we saw a very bemused whale, a great sailing ship, several buildings, some farm machinery, and a number of trees and terrified animals. Everything went the same way, round and round and ever upward, until it reached the funnel, where it vanished into the lightning.

By this time even Astute's curiosity had given way to foreboding, and it was his suggestion that we lash ourselves to rings on the deck, which if nothing else would prevent our being thrown from our craft if the ride got any rockier. As we rose higher and higher, drew closer and closer to the eager lightning, I must have been the only one who didn't expect to die in that bright canopy. I alone knew the true end of one of us, and that the others would be there to see it.

Our way of escape was unsuspected. There must have been some weak point just below the neck of the funnel, for as we neared it we noticed debris, and some of our travelling companions, disappearing into the wall, and when we came to that place we too were drawn in. As we sailed through, the kettle tipped and turned so many ways that nothing untethered could have remained on board. Once we were outside, the water devil flung us from it as if with distaste, flung us so high we passed through clouds, startling many a bird on the wing.

And then the Poppykettle began the long arc of its descent through open sky, and even I began to wonder about our fate. For far below us and stretching off into every distance lay hundreds of strange iridescent islands in a vast sun-spattered lagoon. Nothing could survive such a long fall onto one of those islands. And if we landed in the water...

THE EGG THAT WASN'T

AS IT WAS WE MERELY got another good soaking, though we were badly shaken. Andante had the worst of it, but we guessed he was unconscious long before we hit the water. Cuts and bruises like those could only be gained from being flung about in the hold of a spinning kettle. 'You should have stayed on deck with us,' Astute told him as he stirred. 'You missed a treat.' Andante just groaned.

It is very beautiful here. The islands are mostly coral and the blue of the water is so vivid it dazzles the eye. Sometimes the reef is just below the surface and sometimes just above, so we either swim or walk, whichever is convenient. The water is as clear as can be, and if you look down you see what appears to be ocean floor, though I suppose it's merely a lower shelf of coral or rock. And such an array and abundance of creatures live down there! Astute, whose Gift tells him so much, knows the names of most of them. When I point some creature out to him he usually names it without pause. So I can report that I've seen shrimp and crab and sea urchins, anemones and weaving eels, jellyfish and starfish and – oh, a thousand other species, many of them so colourful and bizarre, so absurd-looking, that it's astonishing that they could exist outside of the imagination.

It's probably just as well there's so much to see, because it seems unlikely that we'll ever leave here. Something must have struck the Poppykettle during our encounter with the water devil, for a crack has appeared in the bowl, a crack so deep that we can see through it. At sea, water would rush in and quickly sink us. But even on land we must sleep somewhere, so we've dragged the kettle up onto the coral, close to a giant clam which seems to have attached itself to the reef.

We were on the reef about a week before we realized that we had not, as we supposed, come there by chance. We might never have discovered this at all if not for Andante. And to think, Aloof doubted the usefulness of Andante's Gift! El Niño knew very well what the Whistler would do when his moment came.

He'd been recuperating slowly from his injuries, playing up a bit in the hope of gaining sympathy. He got none from Don Avante or Astute, but I took him the occasional bowl of poppy tea and sat with him sometimes, and he smiled feebly at me and called me his angel of mercy. But one day he forgot to be unwell. It was a fine afternoon, and the air as sweet as sweet. Don Avante and Astute were dozing on the deck of the Poppykettle while I sprawled on the coral gazing down into the clear water. Andante lay on his back nearby, hands under his head, eyes closed, whistling a jolly little thing that made you tap your fingers and toes without thinking. I'd been watching a very striking golden fish swim elegantly back and forth just below me. It had stripes and spiky whiskers, and fins like wings, and long plumes that stood up all along its spine. It wasn't the first time I'd noticed this fellow. Only the day before I'd asked Astute if he knew what it was. A glance had been sufficient. 'Butterfly cod,' he said, and went off to inspect something else. I put my hand into the water and the butterfly cod came up and nuzzled my fingers.

Suddenly there was a movement in the water off to the right and a very different creature came to join us. It was broad and flat, deep red in colour for the most part, with orange and white markings and a patch of tentacles at one end that looked like veined white leaves. But what most attracted me to the newcomer was that it moved in perfect time to Andante's lively tune. I laughed, and at my laugh this astonishing creature began to undulate around the golden fish without missing a single beat.

'What's so funny?'

It was Astute, bleary-eyed from his nap. Having failed to notice Astute's approach but hearing his voice Andante remembered that he was supposed to be unwell and terminated his whistle in order to moan pathetically. Immediately the flat creature in the water lost its rhythm, though it continued to weave elegantly round the butterfly cod.

'What do you make of this?' I said to Astute. 'Andante, keep whistling, same as before.'

Andante coughed feebly. 'I'd rather not if you don't mind. I try to buck up, you know, but I'm still not feeling my best.'

'Please,' I said. 'It's important.'

'Do as she says, you old fraud,' Astute said, gazing down into the water.

'Old fraud yourself,' mumbled Andante, but he started whistling again, a somewhat sadder, weaker whistle now that he had to feign illness, though the creature picked it up at once and began moving along with it.

'What is that?' I asked Astute.

'It's a nudibranch.'

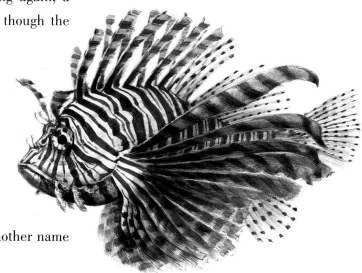

I almost choked. 'You made that up!'

'No, that's what it is, a nudibranch. Also known, I believe, as the Spanish Dancer.'

'The what? Spanish Dancer? Are you sure?'

'Am I usually wrong?' he said smugly.

My heart thumped wildly. 'Astute. Does the butterfly cod have another name too, by any chance?'

'Why yes, now you mention it. It's sometimes called a lionfish... Er, why are you looking at me like that?'

'El Niño's lion-face,' I said. 'Well here we have a lion *fish*. And a dancer. A *Spanish* Dancer.'

'Oh my,' he said. 'Oh my, my, my, my, my.'

'We've found them, Astute. They're here, they've been here all along. The two who'll lead us to the dolphin's egg!'

'Which doesn't exist,' he said, lying down beside me and staring at the two in the water, the one swimming rhythmically round the other to Andante's background whistle.

'Could you speak to them? Ask them if they know where we should look?'

'I could *ask*. No harm in *asking*.'

He sank his face in the water, slowly so as not to frighten them. Bubbles rose from his mouth as he addressed them. Bubbles left theirs as they replied. This went on for some time, with Astute lifting his head for breath every so often. At last he looked at me, water streaming down his face.

'As I keep saying. No such thing as a dolphin's egg.'

My thumping heart stilled. 'But... but I thought...'

He grinned, and water leapt from his beard, spattered my face.

'No such *egg*. The name is given to something else entirely. Something almost as rare.'

'What? Tell me!'

'The black pearl. Black pearls are so rare that many believe they don't exist at all – like the egg of the dolphin. What amazes me is that I didn't know that.'

'Aaaah,' I said with satisfaction. 'Now I see it.'

'What's more, our friends down there say they've been waiting for four people in a cracked pot, to show them where to find it. The pearl, that is. Or perhaps it was four crackpots, can't be sure, it was a bit bubbly at that point.'

'Where then? Where is it?'

'That was going to be my next question.'

79

He plunged his head back into the water. More bubbles rose. Andante again stopped whistling, again gave a moan. The reason this time was that Don Avante was strolling over from the Poppykettle. His shadow fell across Astute, lying there with his head under water.

'What *is* the fellow doing? Things aren't that bad, surely.'

I brought him up to date. By the time I'd finished his eyes were very bright at the prospect of a new adventure.

'So?' he said when Astute came up the last time, gasping. 'Where is it, this rarest of pearls?'

'They tell me that it sits in the maw of its creator.'

'Its creator? And who's that?'

Astute indicated the great shell attached to the coral on which the Poppykettle stood.

'The black pearl may be found inside the giant clam. Very deep inside it. And the clam, they say, has made it known that it will crush to death any creature that tries to steal it. *Any* creature.'

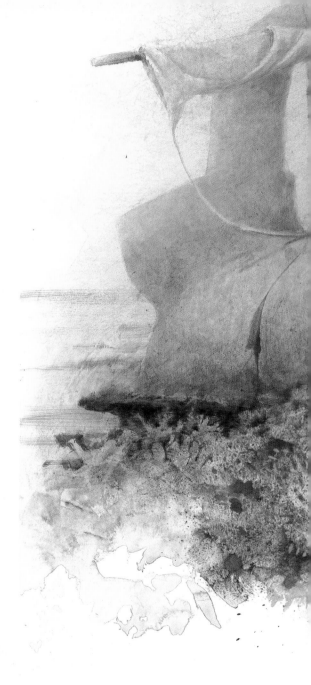

$\int$NTO THE CLAM

ASTUTE THANKED THE BUTTERFLY COD and the nudibranch and they went about their business while we huddled together in whispered counsel, so the clam wouldn't hear.

'It hasn't moved or made a sound since we arrived,' Andante said.

'What do you expect?' barked Don Avante. 'It's a clam.'

'Don't be misled by its stillness,' said Astute. 'The pearl is like its own child. It made it from virtually nothing, applying coat after coat of nacre over a period of years until it was perfect. It will become rather... agitated if we try and remove its pride and joy, count on it.'

'Couldn't you explain?' I said. 'Tell it that El Niño says we must have it?'

'There would be little point. Clams are notoriously antisocial and a law unto themselves. And they don't fear gods.'

'So how do we get our hands on the thing?' Don Avante asked.

'There might be one way. Miserable creatures that they are, they're very ticklish.'

'Ticklish?'

'If you find the right spot. Which I happen to know is a tiny muscle just under the hinge of the shell.'

'And you propose tickling it into a good mood, do you?' sneered Andante. 'Never heard anything so ridiculous in my life. And even if we do manage to snatch the pearl, how far do you think we'll get with the Poppykettle no longer seaworthy?'

'We'll worry about that later,' Don Avante said. 'First, the pearl. It's already ours. We merely have to secure it.'

We made our plans. In the making Andante, by popular vote (three to one, which brought a howl of misery from the one), was ennobled with the title Official Clam Tickler. Before he could take up his new profession, however, there was other work to do. We took down the crossbeam that had supported the sail for so long, and decided to divide it into five equal parts, each about the length of the average Hairy Peruvian. Astute winked at Don Avante and myself and turned to our poor put-upon Whistler.

'My friend, you are surely the most average Hairy Peruvian that ever lived. You shall be our marker!'

For a moment Andante looked affronted, but when we others, containing our laughter, congratulated him on the honour that had been bestowed on him he cocked his chin proudly and cast himself upon the ground beside the beam, his

83

feet at one end of it. Astute marked the beam at his head; then Andante rearranged himself, aligning his feet with the mark while a second was made. When the five sections were marked out we took axes from the hold and set about slicing the beam up. A length about half Andante's height was left over. We had no use for this and let it lie, unaware that it would prove invaluable before we were done.

We laid the five pieces of wood in front of the clam and Andante went round the back with a broom of twigs and instructions to count slowly to two hundred before getting to work. Astute positioned himself before the closed shell and attempted to engage its host in conversation, addressing it as 'Honourable Clam', 'Most Intelligent Mollusc', and so on. Receiving nothing for his pains he talked about the weather and the tides and, almost as an afterthought, asked if the creature had ever heard of something known as a dolphin's egg. At this the clam twitched sharply, but even Astute had no way of telling if it was in response to the query or to an impatient Andante rushing his two hundred to get it over with. A low rumble came from deep within the shell.

'Stomach-ache or language?' Don Avante said.

'If the latter,' Astute replied, 'it's beyond my –'

He broke off because the rumbling noise was growing louder. Then the shell quivered and opened the merest crack, like a mouth about to grin. We leaned forward. The rumbling and the quivering stopped. The shell snapped shut. We leaned back.

'Andante,' Don Avante murmured. 'Useless, utterly useless.'

But then the shell started to quiver again, shake rather, for this was far more energetic; as was the rumbling – higher in pitch, like a strangulated chortle – and once more the two halves of the shell parted. Once more we leaned forward. This time the shaking and rumbling did not stop, the shell did not close.

'Think it's working,' I said.

'Think it is,' said Astute.

Soon the shell was shaking in near hysteria. Don Avante took back what he'd said about Andante. Helpless mirth rippled through the creature and with every fresh wave it opened up a bit more, until, thanks to the lustrous surface of the upper shell, which reflected the exterior light, we beheld a rolling blue plain within.

'See the egg, anyone?' Don Avante said, straining his old eyes. 'Pearl, I should say.'

'No,' I said. 'It's probably at the back, where it's darkest.'

'You know, we ought to get in there before it loses its sense of humour,' Astute said.

'Yes,' said Don Avante, stroking his beard. 'I suppose we ought.'

Just then the top half of the shell jumped up and a great guffaw burst forth. The hair on three Hairy Peruvian heads stood on end. Gazing upon that glistening blue landscape while eerie billows of clamish laughter echoed round the shell I wished fervently that Aloof was with us. He would have leapt inside at once, run straight across the fleshy plain, snatched the pearl, and brought it out in less time than it takes to brew a bowl of poppy tea. But Aloof wasn't there...

85

I climbed onto the rim of the lower shell.

'Arnica, what are you doing!' Don Avante cried.

'This is our chance,' I said. 'It could close again at any moment.'

'Yes, but you're not going in there. Help me up!'

'No. Two at least are needed here to see to the props.'

'Oh, I'm sure Astute could manage without –'

'Grandfather, I'm younger and faster. Please stay here.'

I jumped down on the other side, where I found the flesh unexpectedly soft underfoot, like soggy mud or thick wet seaweed. Don Avante protested, then offered a word or two of caution as I went further in. After a few steps I learned how to measure my stride and best place my feet on that unpleasant floor. The sound the clam made was nothing like laughter now; more like the choking of a human with a bone stuck in his gullet. The blue flesh began to throb. Spidery veins rippled and flexed. Avenues of hairs sprang up like knives. The clam was aware of me, very much aware, and not glad of my company.

'Let's hope they hold, that's all!'

I glanced back. The first two props were in place, holding apart the upper and lower sections of the great shell, which shuddered dreadfully with the effort to crush them. It was like looking out of a living cave whose mouth, straining to close, shook with fury when thwarted. Don Avante and Astute rammed the third, fourth and fifth props in. 'The instant anything goes wrong, Arnica,' Don Avante said, 'you head this way at once, d'you hear?'

'I hear.'

THE PRICE OF THE SECOND PRIZE

FURTHER IN I WENT, and further yet, in a trudging, ungainly lope, wishing once again that Aloof was there, but at my side now rather than on his own. His courage was always greater than mine – courage or foolhardiness – and those eyes of his would have penetrated the gloom without any trouble.

But eventually my ordinary eyes saw what they were searching for, and I approached, in my heavy-footed way, and stood before it. It was as round as the sun, and as big, though as dark as the sun is bright. Yet there was a faint glow to it. The myriad tiny overlapping crystals that made up its surface lent it a lustre, a sheen, a secret light born of unfathomable blackness that I wished I had time to stand and admire. I put my arms round the great pearl and lifted. It budged hardly at all, but a terrible howl bounded around the shell as the clam realized what I'd come for. I lifted again, with every bit of strength in my body.

88 *SSCCCCHHHHLOOOOOP!!!*

I had it! But so much bigger did it seem now that my arms supported it, and so heavy was it, that it seemed impossible that I'd be able to carry it as far as I must. I set off through that disgusting pulp with the pearl in my arms.

'Oh well done, child, well *done*!' Don Avante shouted across the great blue plain. 'But hurry! Hurry!'

'I'm doing my best,' I muttered.

But a moment later such a noise came from the far-too-distant opening that I almost dropped my burden. All five of the props were splintering as the clam began to win its bitter struggle to close. I saw Astute dart away and return with the last length of wood, the small piece, then he and Don Avante were forcing it into the reduced gap, near the centre. The frustrated clam shook with rage and its gaping mouth – as I'd come to think of it – strained more desperately than ever to clamp shut and seal me in.

It was then that an awful realization came to me. I'd been here before. I had already trudged through this sickening flesh-swamp towards an angry mouth-shape divided by fractured stumps of wood. It was the prophecy, the one I'd kept tucked away inside and tried to forget about: the vision of the future in which the second of us was to die. It was coming true.

No! It mustn't happen! I wouldn't let it!

Where the strength came from I don't know, but I now moved towards the opening more swiftly than should have been possible with such a weight in my arms, on such an unhelpful road. Yet the pearl grew heavier and more cumbersome with every step, and soon I began to slow again, and all the while the shell bore down on the six stakes until even the freshest of them, the smallest, was half its former height. I wasn't going to make it. I'd never get out in time – not alone. Don Avante saw this.

'Hold on, my love! Don't fret, I'm coming!'

'No!' I shrieked. 'No, you mustn't! Stay where you are!'

My urgency startled him into hesitation. Astute caught him by the arm. 'She's right. We can't risk you. Stay here, I'll go.'

Don Avante shook him off. 'I am still Elder here and will decide who does what. Steady the props!'

He climbed in, and everything... everything... everything fell into place, bit by bit by bit: the way he stumbled on entering, kicked the fleshy ground before proceeding, held his hands out to me as we drew close. I beseeched him repeatedly to get out before it was too late, but the pearl was so heavy and the way so difficult that my warnings and pleas must have sounded very feeble. When we met he took a side of the pearl, relieving me considerably, and we went on, carrying it between us. It was all happening exactly as I'd seen it in my vision, and nothing I did or said or wished made the slightest difference.

We were almost at the mouth when the five original props gave way. A rasp of triumph raced around the interior as the two halves of the shell crashed together – almost. The sixth and last was bent and badly reduced but it held the shell lips apart by the smallest amount.

'Can you squeeze through, Arnica?'

'No, Grandfather. You first.'

'*Obey* me, girl! Don't *argue*!'

I stepped back, let go of the pearl, forcing him to drop it.

'Arnica, what do you think you're doing?!'

'Leave it! I don't care about it! It's more important to get you out!'

'Leave it? After all this? Never!'

He leaned over the pearl, managed with enormous effort to lift it on his own. Very little light found its way in now, but enough to pick out the bits of splintered wood that had fallen inside. I snatched a sharp piece and began jabbing at the soft flesh. The shell jumped in shock or pain. Opened a fraction more.

'Good!' Don Avante gasped. 'Now step aside!'

I did so, and he ran awkwardly towards the slit with the pearl in his arms; heaved it at the gap. But the space was too narrow and the pearl lodged there. It looked as if our efforts were going to prove in vain, but then Astute, on the other side, was pulling, tugging, and suddenly the pearl was through, and there was a yelp as it landed on his foot.

'Now you!' I rushed at Don Avante, intending to push him after the pearl. But he must have been expecting it, for he jumped back.

'After you, Granddaughter, after you or not at all!'

'But you don't understand! You *have* to go first! I've seen what will happen if you –'

A hollow thudding sound drowned me out. It came from the top of the upper shell, outside. Whatever it was it seemed to enrage the clam further for it gave a furious roar and the flesh under our feet bucked and sent us flying in opposite

91

directions, Don Avante away from the opening, me towards it. Hands reached for me, grabbed me, dragged me out protesting.

'Astute, no! Don Avante's still in there!'

'I realize that, now let's concentrate on getting *him* out, shall we?'

The thudding noise turned out to be Andante on top of the shell, striking it with the handle of his tickling broom.

'Andante, stop!' I shouted. 'You're making it even angrier!'

He stopped. 'Sorry. Thought it would distract it.'

I seized another piece of broken wood, leaned in the opening, stabbed at the flesh. The clam gave a hideous squeal and the shell flew open. The last prop dropped out. Now there was nothing to keep the two halves apart. Don Avante made a dive for the opening. I reached for him. His palm slapped mine. Our fingers hooked. I pulled, dimly aware of Astute nearby trying to wedge something into the shell – the broom, which Andante had thrown down. I had a fair grip on Don Avante's hand, almost had him out, but then the lower part of the shell reared up in a last effort to thwart us, and the broom flew uselessly out, while Andante, who'd been trying to find a way down, slid off with a yell and a thud. Don Avante's hand and mine parted company. He slipped on some oily liquid seeping from the flesh I'd been jabbing. Then the lower shell fell once more and he began slithering feet first towards the opening. Astute and I each caught an ankle and tugged. We had him half out when the upper shell smashed down in triumph.

Sliced Don Avante in two.

THE UNCHOSEN LAND

UNABLE TO COAX or bully the clam into opening up again and releasing Don Avante's body, we rolled the pearl across the coral and round the far side of the Poppykettle so that we wouldn't have to look at the creature that had killed him. I hated the clam, longed to harm it in some way, but Astute reminded me that we were the villains here. If we hadn't stolen the pearl the clam had lovingly nurtured for years Don Avante would still be with us. True as it was, my grief was too great for easy forgiveness.

'One will fall to the angry mouth,' I said. '*That* was the mouth.'

'It seems so,' said Astute, gazing absently out to sea. But then a new note entered his voice, a rather excited note. 'Arnica, remind me of the second part of the verse. Three will leap to the...?'

'Why?'

'Just say it for me. Please.'

93

'*Three will leap to the meeting ground*

Where fear springs at the dark

Where painted past seeks –'

'That'll do,' he said. 'Do you know,' and he laughed, 'do you know, I've just had a rather amusing thought.'

'Amusing?' I said bleakly. 'Is this the time?'

'Poor choice of words. But we have our dolphin's egg. It seems to me that what we could do with now is...'

He walked briskly to the edge of the coral and began waving his arms about and shouting very loudly – not words, though: sounds. Sounds which meant nothing to Andante and me, but which clearly made sense to the dolphin that had been passing by, for it replied in like fashion and turned towards us. Astute told the dolphin about the crack in the Poppykettle which had left us stranded. The dolphin was sympathetic. He was on his way to a family gathering in the south, he said, an annual get-together. He would be happy to give us a lift if that direction suited us. At this, Astute roared with such delight that our recent tragedy might not have occurred.

'Three will leap to the meeting ground!' he cried. 'And what are we about to do?'

'Oh now,' Andante said, 'I don't know about leaping...'

'Then walk, if that's your preference.'

We accepted the dolphin's offer. Even if Astute was wrong, better an unknown destination than none at all. When asked how he could carry us, the dolphin suggested that we tie the Poppykettle onto his head. I thought he was joking and my giggle danced away across the coral, to return and warm my cheeks in the dolphin's wounded silence. We had nothing like enough rope to go round his great head, so we cut the sail into strips and knotted them together. As a sail it had had its day anyway.

It would have been unthinkable to leave the pearl behind after all that had happened, even though we had no idea what to do with it, so, lowering the kettle into the water, we rolled it onto the deck and threw a net over it to hold it. The dolphin was patience itself during the next manoeuvre, lying perfectly still in the water while I swam beneath him with the sail-rope and tossed it up on the far side to Astute and Andante, who secured it across the kettle. This done we returned to the coral to pay our last respects to our valiant leader. The haunting melody of Andante's *Last Whistle for an Old Friend* almost broke my heart.

In sombre mood we climbed up onto the Poppykettle and told the dolphin that we were ready.

At first he swam on the surface for our sake, but it was his nature to leap, and when he did this without warning we were all three reduced instantly to quivering bags of nerves. Our new friend apologized, we calmed ourselves, and a minute later he did it again. But in a while, seeing that we made better progress that way, we gave him permission to continue and soon were enjoying our ride so much that we wondered why everyone didn't travel like that.

'Leaping or not,' Andante said to Astute, 'I don't see how this can have anything to do with El Niño's verse. You hailed the dolphin on impulse. Pure

coincidence that he's going to some family do.'

Astute would have none of it. 'If I were you, Andante, I wouldn't be so sure that anything in El Niño's world is as random as we, in our conceit, like to imagine.'

'Well if you're right,' I said, 'he's playing with us.'

'Playing with us? Oh, I wouldn't say that.'

'No? Once upon a time, if the legend is true, our people were dolls made for sacrifice to him. I think he accepted the sacrifice and made walking-talking toys of us for his personal entertainment.'

He patted my hand. 'You're upset, Arnica. You've had a trying time of it. Things'll work out in the end, you see if they don't.'

I snatched my hand away angrily. 'It won't work out for my brother or for Don Avante. It won't work out for all the others he took. And even if we do find our way to this new land of his, we'll still be his playthings. He'll be our master for as long as we live.'

We passed much of the journey in sleep, strapped into our bunks to avoid being thrown all over the place during the dolphin's leaps. During those many days and nights the crack in the kettle lengthened and broadened, so that by the time we reached our destination it was large enough for us to step through without stooping or breathing in.

The land we had come to was so massive it seemed to have no end one way or the other. As we approached the dolphin spoke to Astute, who translated.

'He says there are hidden rocks here and that he must be careful. This is

Indented Head, so called because an ancestor of his ran into some of them —
dented his head.'

The amiable dolphin bore us past the rocks without denting anything, into a
calm bay, and a sheltered nook in one corner of it, where he suggested that now
would be a very good time to remove the Poppykettle. His gathering place was
situated at the other arm of the bay and his life wouldn't be worth living, he said,
if certain younger members of his family saw him with a clay pot on his head.

We untied the sail-rope and, assisted by our friend's admirable nose, set the
kettle as far back from the water as we could. While we were doing this one of
the sacks of poppyseed fell through the crack and burst open on the ground. With
more important things to think about, we left the scattered seeds where they fell.

The night of our arrival. Very late. Astute and Andante are asleep in their bunks.
I couldn't sleep and came up here to sit on the neck of the spout and write
this by the light of the stars. Feel so strange tonight. Foreboding and expectation
in equal measure. We have no idea what we'll find in this new country, or even
where it is. Have we reached World's Edge without knowing it? Before he went
to bed Astute suggested that I seek a future for us. I refused. I never want to
use my Gift again. Besides, I don't need it to tell me the most important thing:
that the Poppykettle has sailed for the last time; that it will never carry us from
this shore or any other. Whether or not it was part of El Niño's plan that we
end up here — and whatever we feel about it — we must make our home in this
unchosen land.

Astute's Conclusion

FEAR OF THE OUTER WORLD

ARNICA HAS ASKED ME to bring this history of our adventures to a close. The reason is that it was I who discovered that the Unchosen Land was indeed the country El Niño had in mind for us. This is how it came about.

The morning after our arrival I was woken by a truly horrendous noise which, after jumping off my bunk believing we were under attack, I realized was one of Andante's barbaric snores. How Arnica can sleep through that man's racket mystifies me, but she did not stir. I shuffled to the crack in the side of the kettle to see what our first day in this new land looked like. It was a bright one – the sun had been up for some time – but it wasn't the weather that made me start. I recalled the prediction Arnica had made as we were about to leave the old shore, that at some point in the future we would meet a white pelican. That point had been reached.

My first impulse was to wake her, but she was sleeping so peacefully that it seemed a shame, so I stepped through the crack and bid the pelican good morning. When he returned my greeting I noted with interest that he spoke the same language as the pelicans of the old country, though with a rather quaint accent. He had been waiting for us to stir for some time, he said. 'I did not wish to disturb you. I know you Small Ones. You are a very private people – most of you.'

'There are others like us here?' I said in surprise.

'Why yes, didn't you know? Well, I'm sure you'll come across them before long. They're a fearful, scurrying lot, but they may venture out for one like themselves. Forgive me, sir, but I've been looking at that cargo of yours. From what I can see of it, it's a very fine thing.' He indicated the net-covered pearl on the deck of the kettle. 'Does it have some... purpose?'

'That remains to be seen,' I answered, resolving to say no more till I knew him better. As it happened I didn't need to.

'If you are at a loss for a use to put it to,' he said, 'I may be able to suggest one...'

And this is what he told me. Quite near to where we'd parked the Poppykettle there lives a proud and peaceful community of humans who call themselves Oldshadows. There is an ancient prophecy among the Oldshadows that a fair-skinned race will one day settle their land without invitation or blessing. They call these future invaders Lilywhites and dread the day of their coming, for they will bring about great and unwanted changes. However, there is a second legend, a companion to the first, which avers that three Small Ones will bring a dolphin's egg from across the Great Water. If the dolphin's egg is placed without condition inside the Black Stump, the second legend declares, Oldshadow peace will be preserved for fifty years more.

'What is this Black Stump?' I enquired.

'I'll show it to you,' the pelican said. 'Climb on my back.'

I told him that I couldn't leave without informing my companions, to which he replied that we could be there and back before they missed me. I was deliberating on this when I noticed something that turned me, quite without ceremony, into a slack-jawed imbecile. The poppyseeds that had fallen out of the kettle upon our arrival last evening had taken root overnight – and were already growing!

'This land of yours seems to welcome our seed,' I said in wonder.

'It may be so,' the pelican said. 'It welcomes some. Are you coming or not?'

So, leaving the others to their slumbers, I climbed on his back and he flew me to the place of the Black Stump. And what was it? Why, nothing more than the hollow bowl of a burnt-out tree.

'And this is of some... significance?' I said dubiously.

'It is of great significance. It is the Meeting Ground. It is where –'

'Excuse me, did you say Meeting Ground?'

'Indeed. The Black Stump stands where north meets south and east meets west. Once it was a tall and healthy tree from which all journeys began, but many years ago lightning struck it and reduced it to its present condition. Yet still the

Oldshadows gather here to... Ah! It seems that we're not alone.'

The remains of the old tree stood in the middle of a barren white plain encircled by rocks. In some of the rocks there were holes like small caves, and poking out of several of the caves were faces that had not been there a minute before; faces of sensible size, staring at me – as well they might. I cried out in recognition, and my cry was returned by twenty or more gaping mouths while the rest were struck too dumb to utter a sound.

'Astute? No! It can't be, you're dead.'

'Not quite. A little the worse for wear perhaps, but...' I turned to the white pelican. 'I take it these are the Small Ones you mentioned.'

'They are. It seems you are acquainted after all.'

'Oh we are! By El Niño, we are!' I clapped my hands with delight. 'My friends! Come out, let me see you! Austere, is that you? Adamant? Arpeggio? Why, Arrant, you too! And Anon! And the twins, Also and Also! This is wonderful! No, it's... it's unbelievable!'

And out they came, in twos and threes and dribs and drabs, not only from the little caves but from many a dark place within the rocks; and I can't tell you how my heart swelled to see them all. And then we were embracing and singing and dancing and... well, generally behaving in a very undignified fashion.

While this reunion was going on the white pelican took it upon himself to return to the Poppykettle for Arnica and Andante. When he brought them to the Black Stump I said: '*This* is the place! *This* is the Meeting Ground of El Niño's verse!' Their wonder was as great as mine when they saw who and how many I

103

had discovered, and the hugging and prancing began all over again – and the questions.

'Where's Askew? Is he here?'

'Oh, he's about somewhere. Still hiding, probably.'

'And Allegro, Arnago, dear old Aplomb?'

'Aplomb is fatter and lazier than ever now, rarely gets up before midday, but Arnago and Allegro went off fishing before first light. They've found a little tucked-away stream where they feel safe.'

'You seem very nervous of this country,' said Andante, nervous himself now and glancing about in case he'd missed some threat.

'With good cause,' was the reply. 'There are painted Tall Ones here, and many other peculiar creatures besides, all speaking quite indecipherable tongues and surely wishing us harm.'

'We saw you carried off by a great wave,' Arnica said. 'How could you possibly have survived that, and come so far?'

It was my crusty old friend Austere who cleared this up for them, though I had already heard the tale. 'We too thought our time had come, but as we were swept out to sea we found that the wave was a chariot driven by El Niño himself. He conveyed us here with all speed, informing us that the old shore was the land of our infancy and that this is where we'll find our maturity – or not, it's up to us apparently. He cruelly left without telling us what we should do, or even what to fear.'

104   'You didn't used to be as fearful as this,' I said, puzzled.

'Of course not,' said Alack. 'We knew what to expect back home. But this is the Outer World. There's always something to fear in the Outer World, the Maker made certain we understood that from our first breath.'

'Well, that's one piece of Wisdom I'm pleased not to possess,' I replied. 'El Niño himself breathed life into me before he passed the Gift to Adagio. I have no recollection of being told to fear the world and consequently take my fears as they –'

I stopped because there isn't much point in going on when the people you're addressing suddenly kick up their hind legs and scamper off like frightened rabbits. Arnica, Andante and I could only gape after them in amazement as they burrowed into their caves and crevices and any other dark hidey-hole they could find at short notice. But we soon discovered the reason for their panic. Standing with the white pelican on the high rocks above the Black Stump were two dozen well-nigh naked humans with spears. Dark-skinned Tall Ones painted from brow to toe with outlandish configurations.

THE BOLD ONE

I TURNED TO ARNICA to tell her not to be afraid, and found that she and I were alone. 'What happened to Andante?'

'He went after the others. Can't say I blame him.'

'We'll learn nothing if we all scurry away like that,' I said.

'These are representatives of the Oldshadows I spoke of,' said the pelican from on high. 'I have told them of the arrival of new Small Ones who may have something for them – though of course it's up to you whether you part with the object in question. It must be given freely or the old prophecy may be corrupted.'

Having as yet no idea how Oldshadows speak I greeted them in Hairy Peruvian, supplying our names as credentials. The men did not reply but began threading their way in single file through a narrow pass between the rocks. When they reached our level they reassembled behind the Black Stump. The pelican remained where he was. For what seemed an eternity everyone stood absolutely motionless and silent, like a frozen tableau, but then another figure appeared beside the pelican, a veritable apparition with more markings upon his person than any of his fellows. Circling his head was an embroidered band containing a great crown of feathers, all of them ordinary enough but for a tall purple one at the centre, which simply glowed among the others. Arnica touched my arm.

'Is that what I think it is?'

'I was going to ask you the same thing.' I addressed the pelican. 'This is their leader?'

'It is.'

'Does he speak? Do any of them speak?'

'They speak my language and I speak theirs,' the pelican said. 'Either will do.'

Now the chief of the Oldshadows also descended, slowly and with great dignity, and when he reached the plain he took up a stance in front of his people, some way from us so as not to tower over us. Again I introduced Arnica and myself. The chief did not give his name (later we learnt that Oldshadows value their names too much to hand them out freely to strangers) but he was extremely courteous.

'I am told that you have travelled far, Small Ones.'

'Yes. Across the Great Water, from where the sun rises.'

'I hear it is warm there.'

'Much of the time. Is it warm here, where the sun goes down?'

'Much of the time. In what did you travel?'

'In a kettle made by the old gods for brewing the holy poppy tea.'

'It is appropriate! And do you bring something which might be of interest to Oldshadows?'

'We carry the dolphin's egg of prophecy, which we would be very pleased to present to you and your people as a sign of friendship.'

At this he smiled a little, which made him look far less ferocious. 'I will do you the honour of accepting the gift and your friendship.'

'Tell me,' I said then, 'do you have a Cunmerrie in this country?'

The chief looked puzzled, so I asked him how the splendid purple feather had come into his keeping.

'My friend gave it to me,' he said, as if he thought everyone knew that. 'The bold Small One.'

Now I was puzzled. 'I've seen no bold Small Ones here today.'

'The one of whom he speaks,' the white pelican informed us, 'is not one of those craven scurriers. He arrived later than they and refused to hide away in the dark with them. He built a house for himself in a tree and welcomed all species but those he likes to hunt. Until he came,' the pelican went on, 'the Oldshadows thought the Small Ones were the Lilywhites of prophecy, and that they would somehow bring an end to their peaceful existence in spite of their diminutive size. The bold one put their minds at rest by making them a gift of something they admired.'

'The purple feather?' Arnica said.

'The purple feather,' said the white pelican.

110   Arnica and I glanced at one another with mounting excitement.

'Where is he then, this tree-dwelling friend-maker?' I asked. 'If he does not hide like the others how is it that he doesn't show himself to us?'

'Because these days,' said a voice from behind us, 'he prefers to find out what's going on before barging in.'

Arnica and I whirled about. The 'bold one' stood atop the rocks grinning his silly head off. His clothing was as skimpy as the Oldshadows', and like them he bore painted marks all over his body. He also carried a spear, which had never been his habit before.

'Aloof?' I said. 'Is it really you?'

Arnica needed no confirmation. As the painted boy jumped down she ran to him and clasped him to her so hard it's a wonder the lad's ribs didn't crack. But a second later she was holding him at arm's length, scowling furiously.

'What is the meaning of this? How dare you be here when you're supposed to be lost at sea? I've been mourning you for weeks. You might have let us know!'

'How could I?' he said, 'I –'

'And when I catch up with you at last, when I finally track you down, what do I find? Why, that you've gone native! Look at you! Hairy Peruvians do not strip off their clothes and paint their bodies, Aloof. And they don't live in trees either. You should be *ashamed* of yourself!'

During the last of this the boy's grin returned, and as his sister finished he said: 'And to think, I quite missed being nagged and bossed about and put in my place. I must be mad!'

111

THE FULFILMENT OF PROPHECIES

LATER, ALOOF TOLD US what had happened after the Cunmerrie feather carried him into the storm-cloud. El Niño had indeed been waiting in the cloud, but not for the feather alone. He wanted Aloof too. Once the cloud was well away from the Poppykettle, he placed Aloof in a reed boat with the feather for a sail and commanded a wind to blow him to the new country, where his wave-chariot had already borne fifty-nine of our people. The first acquaintance Aloof made on his arrival was the white pelican, who seems to make it his business to personally greet all newcomers in order to ascertain whether their influence on his country is likely to be good or bad. Of course, Aloof was delighted to find our people still alive, but he was less pleased to learn that, without a strong leader, they had become a very nervous bunch. He at once set to making friends with those they most feared, not least the Oldshadows. It wasn't till he'd given the feather to the chief as a token of his regard that he realized that he'd done precisely what El

112

Niño had wanted: shown the Oldshadows that the Small Ones were not their enemy, thus preparing the way for our coming with the so-called dolphin's egg.

Aloof was sad to hear of Don Avante's fate but quick to realize that I was now the oldest living Hairy Peruvian, even counting those who had come here before us; and he was the first to address me as Don Astute. I was touched by this, but when he went further and called me Grandfather the tears simply sprang to these foolish old eyes. I've always had a liking for Aloof, wild as he sometimes is.

I asked the white pelican if he would be so kind as to bring the black pearl to the Meeting Ground. Arnica and Andante went with him to release it from the net, and when they returned we presented the pearl to the chief with some ceremony so that the handing over would be remembered and spoken of in afteryears. The Oldshadows placed their long-awaited dolphin's egg inside the Black Stump and thus guaranteed themselves fifty more years of peace and harmony. In return for the gift, the chief promised protection to all Hairy Peruvians for the duration, and beyond if it could be managed.

'It's done,' Arnica said then. 'All of it. Just as El Niño foretold.'

'Done?' said Aloof. 'What's done?'

'Five shall embark and two be lost

One will race to the Shadows (you, to the Oldshadows)

One will fall to the angry mouth

And three will count the cost.

Three will leap to the meeting ground

Where fear springs at the dark

Where painted past seeks prophecy
And names emerge, undrowned.'

'Oh that,' Aloof said. 'Yes, I suppose it is.'

Next morning Andante, Arnica, Aloof and I were sitting quietly together on the deck of the kettle sipping bowls of poppy tea. We've grown used to our small company and three of us at least have yet to reaccustom ourselves to crowds.

'One thing I don't understand,' Arnica said. 'El Niño's all-powerful, right? He could have seized the Cunmerrie's feather and the dolphin's egg and given them to the Oldshadows himself. Why get us to do it? And what would have happened if we'd failed to?'

'I've been thinking about that,' I said, 'and have concluded that he wanted to see what we were made of; whether we're still, deep down, creatures of wood and cloth and human hair, or if we're made of sterner stuff. Imagine how things might have gone if we had not secured the feather and the egg. The Oldshadow prophecy would not have come true and that noble race would have been denied its last fifty years of peace before the Lilywhites come. As for the fifty-nine, they would probably have lived out their days in their caves and hovels, shivering with fear of everything that moves and doesn't move. It seems that we were really quite important.'

'I could have told you that,' said Andante.

Aloof smirked. 'Oh you could, could you?'

'Certainly. If I'd a mind to. But I never had much time for idle speculation. My Gift is far more amusing than mere *Wisdom*.'

So saying, he began to whistle the most tuneless thing that ever passed his lips.

Our people were very taken with the Poppykettle when we showed it to them, and impressed that it could have brought us all this way without El Niño piloting it. Something else impressed them too. The poppyseeds that had sprouted within hours of falling upon the ground grew so rapidly that in a matter of days we had a plot of poppies in glorious bloom. Encouraged by this, we cast down other seeds that we'd brought with us from the old shore. The ground accepted these also, and before many meals were consumed an unruly garden had sprung up about the kettle. So delighted were they with this, and so improved was their self-esteem now that the Oldshadows had publicly promised their friendship and protection, that the fifty-nine abandoned their gloomy caves and drew up plans for proper houses to be built around the Poppykettle.

While they set about building their new homes we four filled in the great crack with clay, and sank sturdy foundations to keep the kettle from toppling over in a high wind. We are now building a roofed dwelling beneath the handle and making a sheltered terrace of the deck. Our final task will be to decorate the interior of the bowl. We've agreed that it will make an ideal meeting house. What better or more appropriate place for the last Hairy Peruvians to congregate and decide how best to deal with our future in this rather promising new country of ours?

Years on the End of the Beginning

(Aloof's Last Words)

FIFTY YEARS HAVE PASSED since this history was written. They've been good years, though a bit on the quiet side for my taste. Arnica and I did go adventuring once (with Andante of all people) and very nearly met a nasty end or two along the way, but my dear sister says that if I write it down I'm in trouble. That means that I can't even tell you why she's so touchy about it, but never mind.

We have acquired many Skills to complement our Gifts over this half century, and have come to feel that Hairy Peruvians can do anything they put their minds to. El Niño gave us enough years of peace here to learn what we could never have learned on the shore of our birth: that people of sensible size have a true place upon this flat earth.

A true place, but not it seems this very patch. For Lilywhites have begun arriving in great numbers and we can no longer wander where we please. Their ridiculous great feet are everywhere – and their prying eyes. Our friends the

117

Oldshadows are nervous about them too, for different reasons. They say the Lilywhites are dangerous, that they spoil everything they touch, and what they don't understand they destroy. The Oldshadows will not be able to protect us from such a breed. Because of this it was decided at last night's meeting in the Poppykettle that we will venture inland, where Lilywhite feet have not yet trodden, and seek a new home there. We won't be taking the kettle, of course. That unlikely object has served us well over this half century, first as the craft that carried us here against all odds, then as a comfortable home and meeting house. Before we leave we plan to tow it out to the deep and send it to a dignified end. Andante is composing a special whistle for the occasion. He calls it *The Poppykettle Farewell*.

As for this history, we hope it will be found some day, but an early finding could make life difficult for us so we're going to hide it away. Don Astute is making a copy so that if one is not discovered the other might yet be found. Each will be placed in a sealed box along with one or two mementos and some of the drawings Arnica made during our journey here. One box will be buried in the soil on which we've lived so pleasantly for five decades. A grandson of the white pelican who welcomed us has offered to carry the other to a great island he knows, which he says is called Tasland. It may be that by the time one or other of the boxes is unearthed we will all have passed on, but it's possible that a few of us will still be about, for Hairy Peruvians are a long-lived race. Look there, O reader! What was that at the corner of your eye? A person of sensible size? Oh, surely not, surely not. But it may have been. It may very well have been.

VISIT TO A MUSEUM

THEY HADN'T BEEN HERE since they were boys. Not since their parents brought them on a special visit to see their find under glass. Time for another special visit, they'd decided, now they had growing kids of their own. The long glass-topped cabinets looked exactly the same, if a bit smaller and older, but the stuff had been moved to one at the far end, deep in the slanting afternoon shadow.

'Here they are, Andy,' Rick said. 'Look, Angela.'

The two men and their children huddled over the smeared glass.

'Found them when we weren't much older than you,' said Tom.

Hushed tones, as at a shrine. The boy and girl gazed at the little box, permanently open; the half dozen minuscule papers (token selection from the archive); the ancient drawings hardly bigger than a thumb nail; the tiny shirt with squiggles and dots on the back; the casual scatter of black seeds. They'd been hearing about the Big Find since they were knee-high to a koala. In their families it had been like playing golf on the Moon. Amazing there wasn't some jumpy old black and white film of it. And this was it? *This* was what they'd been on about all those years? Andy and Angela exchanged pitying glances, hoiked their eyes to the ceiling, wandered off.

'Such is fame,' sighed Tom.

Rick shrugged, equally disappointed but more by the display itself than the kids' reaction. Finding the box in the Longford barns had always felt like the high point of their lives, but the way their great discovery had been sidelined, shoved into the shadows here...

'Hey, man, look at this. Jeez, the nerve!'

The glass had got a little scratched over the years and the creeping sunlight reflected uncomfortably. Rick squinted.

'What am I looking at?'

'The notice. The disclaimer.'

Tom pointed at a neat yellow card below the exhibit.

WHILE THE SO-CALLED POPPYKETTLE MATERIAL HAS BEEN CARBON-DATED AS MID-16TH CENTURY IN ORIGIN AND OF PRIMITIVE SOUTH AMERICAN MANUFACTURE, SOME EXPERTS HAVE EXPRESSED DOUBTS ABOUT ITS AUTHENTICITY ON THE GROUNDS THAT PEOPLE OF SUCH LIMITED STATURE (THE PROVINCE OF FANTASY AND FAIRYTALE) ARE UNLIKELY TO HAVE EVOLVED INTO INTELLIGENT LIFE-FORMS.

Rick snorted angrily. 'In other words they think it's all fake.'

'So what does that make us?' Tom said. 'I'll tell you what it makes us: fools or hoaxers, take your pick.'

'Experts! What do they know?'

'Yeah, what the hell do they kn –'

A crash from the next room, followed by a yell.

'Andy, that you?'

'Angela?'

'You can't leave 'em for a minute. Better see what's up.'

When the men had gone there was complete stillness in the room for some minutes. Then two small figures emerged from the shadow they'd tucked themselves into in a panic, tiptoed back along the glass.

'Wonder what those Tall Ones were saying?' said the female.

'Who cares? Tall Ones never say anything worth hearing.' They gazed again at the items under glass beneath their feet. 'Wouldn't mind knowing what it says on the card though.'

'Yes. If only Don Astute were still alive...'

There was something childlike about these two – not surprisingly, for they'd been fashioned as children long ago, and their kind's flesh does not age the way human flesh ages.

Yet there was something almost elderly about them too. A modest price, perhaps, for four and a half centuries of life.

'I can't believe we came all that way for this,' the man-boy said.

'I just wanted to see what they'd done with our things. You didn't have to come.'

'Might have been worth the trip, then I'd have missed out. Just as well the other box doesn't seem to have been discovered or you'd have me tracking it down too.'

His sister, staring down, was suddenly filled with a terrible sadness.

'It's like... like it belonged to someone else. Someone who died a long time ago.'

'Well, that's the past for you. Never think about it myself. Look, can we go now? We have a pelican to catch. Promised to be home by year's end, remember?'

She sighed. 'All right.'

They left the building. Left it gladly in the end. Left not by door, nor window, but by some other way. Some Hairy Peruvian way.